DEAD

Abernethy rubbed a closely shaven cheek. "I've got my own plans, Drennan, concerning Harriman and his bunch. It would seem that most of Broken Ring's troubles are due to him."

"And Red." Cotton jerked a thumb at Donahue. "If Malloy was a real cattleman, Red would have gone a long time ago."

A quick grin came to Abernethy's lips when he glanced at Donahue. "He don't think much of you, does he, Red?"

Donahue's face was a mask of murderous rage. "I don't think much of him, neither. This is the time I've been waiting for. I'm gonna kill you, Cotton."

"Murder is a bad business, Abernethy," Cotton said, "even out here."

"If," Donahue added, "anybody knows about it, which they won't this time." There was the ominous click of Donahue's hammer being drawn back....

WAYNE D. OVERHOLSER

*Twice Winner of the Spur Award
and Winner of
the Lifetime Achievement Award from
the Western Writers of America*

WITHDRAWN

S0-FBA-053

Other *Leisure Books* by Wayne D. Overholser:

WEST OF THE RIMROCK
DRAW OR DRAG
VALLEY OF GUNS
CAST A LONG SHADOW
FABULOUS GUNMAN
STEEL TO THE SOUTH
THE LONE DEPUTY
DESPERATE MAN
THE VIOLENT LAND
THE JUDAS GUN
HEARN'S VALLEY
TOUGH HAND

NORWALK PUBLIC LIBRARY
NORWALK   OHIO

WAYNE D. OVERHOLSER

BUCKAROO'S CODE

LEISURE BOOKS ■ NEW YORK CITY

TO MY SONS
John and Stephen

A LEISURE BOOK®

June 1992

This edition is reprinted by arrangement with MACMILLAN PUBLISHING COMPANY, a division of Macmillan, Inc. by

Dorchester Publishing Co., Inc.
276 Fifth Avenue
New York, NY 10001

If you purchased this book without a cover you should be aware that this book is stolen property. It was reported as "unsold and destroyed" to the publisher and neither the author nor the publisher has received any payment for this "stripped book."

Copyright © MCMXLV, MCMXLVII by Wayne D. Overholser

All rights reserved. No part of this book may be reproduced or transmitted in any form or by any electronic or mechanical means, including photocopying, recording or by any information storage and retrieval system, without the written permission of the Publisher, except where permitted by law.

For further information, contact: Macmillan Publishing Co., Inc., a division of Macmillan, Inc., 866 Third Avenue, New York, NY 10022

The name "Leisure Books" and the stylized "L" with design are trademarks of Dorchester Publishing Co., Inc.

Printed in the United States of America.

Chapter One

The Great Man
Comes to Antioch

IT WAS MID-AFTERNOON WHEN COTTON DRENNAN STEPPED
out of Duke Bellew's barber shop, and loitered for a moment
under the wooden awning as he shaped up a cigarette. He was
the sort of man who belonged on a horse, and somehow it
seemed a little odd for him to be standing on his own two
legs. The sun and wind of the high country had turned his face
a dark bronze, and it formed, when his hat was off, a strange
contrast with his nearly white blond hair. His smooth face
showed no care. This was the day he'd been looking forward
to for a long time, but now that it was here, there was little
satisfaction in it.

Inside the barber shop Cotton had bought a haircut, a shave,
and a bath. A summer's sweating on the range lay behind.
There should have been a great warmth of contentment inside
him as he stood with the fall sun slanting down upon him.
Soon he'd be in a pool game. Then he'd have a thick steak
at Big Nose Charlie's, a drink or so with his friends in the
Empress Saloon, and he'd wind up the day by taking June

Flagg to the dance. He hadn't asked June yet, but he'd get around to it before long.

Yet now, as Cotton stood within minutes of realizing these things he had anticipated so long, he knew that the taste of realization would be flat and without savor. Over-shadowing them in his mind was the dark picture of the brush-covered graves he'd found beside the ashes of Luke Bray's cabin.

Half a block away fat Bill Curry let out a squall. "Lookit, Santiam," Curry cried. "He's standing in front of the barber shop all purtied up."

Santiam Jones was so thin that Curry claimed he couldn't even cast an anemic shadow. Now Santiam cocked his narrow head as he came up to Cotton. He said sourly, "Nope. It ain't Cotton. It's a wooden Indian Duke picked up to scare away trade. Cotton never smelled like this."

"Who ever heard of an Indian with hair the color of this hombre's?" Curry demanded derisively. "You're getting so skinny you can't even cast a good, healthy look."

"All right," Cotton said wearily. "The last time I saw you galoots was over on the other side of Bridger Butte, and you was arguing then. Don't you ever get done?"

"Nope," Santiam Jones said placidly. "There's only one thing to do. We'll go over and have a drink."

"Or two drinks," Bill Curry amended.

"Keno Harriman and his crowd are in the Empress," Santiam said.

"Makes me no never mind," Cotton said. "We don't have to drink with no rag-tailed bunch of gunslick varmints. We'll get to the other end of the bar."

For a moment a feeling of satisfaction filled Cotton as he stood at the bar between Santiam Jones and Bill Curry. Friendship was one of the things that made living worth while. Then Bill Curry said, "Drink up, son. That's good liquor in front of you." And Cotton realized he was thinking again of the graves he'd found beside the charred remnants of Luke Bray's cabin.

Gaunt Santiam Jones permitted himself a smile. "You ought

BUCKAROO'S CODE

to know about that being good liquor, Bill."

Curry ignored Santiam's remark. He said, "Cotton, you think too much."

Again Santiam smiled. "That's one thing nobody will ever accuse you of."

"You ain't no ball of fire between the ears, neither," Curry snapped. "Cotton's got the only brain on Broken Ring."

"Thanks," Cotton said somberly. "Boys, I was just wondering why we're working for Broken Ring. I ain't real fond of Jackson Malloy."

"Well," Curry demanded, "why are we here?"

Cotton put his mind back over his twenty-four years of living. He could hardly remember a time when he had not spent most of his waking hours in the saddle. It showed in his walk, in his six-foot, lean-hipped body. Most of those years had been drifting years that had taken him south from Montana to Arizona, and north again to the high country of central Oregon.

"I don't rightly know," Cotton said finally, "why a man would stay on a spread where he don't like the owner, and hates the ramrod. Gents, that's exactly where I stand. I can't stomach Jackson Malloy, and one of these days I'm gonna have the supreme pleasure of taking a punch at Red Donahue's jaw. I think it's glass, and boys, I'd sure love to bust it."

"There ain't a Broken Ring rider who don't hate Donahue," Santiam Jones said.

Cotton jerked a thumb toward the row of gun-hung men bellied up against the bar at the other end of the mahogany. "That bunch of Keno Harriman's likes Red all right."

"I said riders," Jones growled. "Hell, them ornery sons ain't nothing but perfessional gunslingers. They wouldn't know the front end of a bull from the back."

"Last week," Cotton said somberly, "I rode over to Sand Spring to see Luke Bray. The cabin had been burned. There was two graves in the yard covered over by brush so a man wouldn't see 'em unless he got nosy."

Curry swore softly. "Keno's bunch rode by where me and

Santiam was camped at Bridger Butte."

"A big outfit like Broken Ring can't let sodbusters stay on their range," Santiam said. "Luke had been warned."

"I said two graves," Cotton said quickly.

Jones growled an oath. "He did have a wife, didn't he?"

"Let's go get our time," Curry said. "It's dirty money Jackson Malloy pays, but we've got some coming."

"Not yet." Cotton shook his head. "I ain't ready to move. I like to look at the Sisters and old Jefferson. Never saw purtier mountains in my life. I like to hunt and fish, and this country is sure made to order."

"Wouldn't be June Flagg you really like, would it, son?" Santiam Jones asked slyly.

"Or the huckleberry pies she bakes," Curry added.

"Right on both counts," Cotton admitted. Slowly he turned the filled glass in his fingers, eyes on the amber-shining liquor. "Dammit, boys, what can a man do who don't own nothing but the shirt on his back and the gun on his hip?"

"Did you try asking her?" Jones demanded. "Besides, you failed to mention a roan horse and a saddle."

"I've been doing some thinking," Cotton said gloomily, "since I found those graves. There's Fred Flagg and June on the FF, holding the only watering place on White River for twenty miles. Malloy needs it, but I reckon he ain't pushed Fred because he's kind o' sweet on June himself. But if June won't have him . . ."

"You know damned well she won't," Santiam broke in. "Then there'll be two graves along White River. If that happens, remember you've got a couple of guns to side you."

"Correct," Bill Curry agreed.

"Thanks," Cotton said huskily. "I'll remember that."

They stood in silence for a time, even Bill Curry staring gloomily at the marred top of the mahogany. Then Cotton raised his glass. "I haven't tasted this yet, boys."

"Speak of the devil," Santiam said a moment later. "There he is."

BUCKAROO'S CODE 9

Jackson Malloy had come in, a fat cigar tucked into one corner of his meaty-lipped mouth. He was a heavy-bodied man, and a handsome one by some standards. His eyes were dark, his nose thin and rather sharp, his chin square. Those who didn't know him would have said he was a friendly man; those who did know him knew also that it was only a veneer which he put on like a coat. There were two things in life that Jackson Malloy loved: Jackson Malloy and money. He had spent money on Broken Ring for no better reason than to sell it for more money. This thing, Cotton knew, of spending money to make more money was an art of which Jackson Malloy was a master.

Malloy's eyes ran the length of the bar. All the men along it were Broken Ring men. Those in the front were the gunslingers, their boss, hard-eyed Keno Harriman, standing at the end of the line. Cotton, Curry, and Santiam Jones were at the far end of the mahogany. Malloy's white teeth showed in a smile as he nodded at Cotton. "You boys down there move up a piece."

Luke Bray's burned cabin! The brush-covered graves! Again that gruesome picture crowded back into Cotton's mind as he stepped away from the bar. There would never be a better time to push this thing than right now.

"We ain't drinking with them," Cotton said, jerking a thumb at Keno Harriman.

It was Harriman's way to ignore the buckaroos who rode for Broken Ring, but now he spun toward Cotton, thin face dark with quick fury. "Why not?"

"Buckaroos drink together," Cotton said. "So do hired gunhands."

"What the hell is this?" Malloy's puzzled eyes whipped from Cotton to Harriman and back.

"I just wanted to make things clear," Cotton said as he moved along the bar toward Malloy. "It's your business if you want to hire a bunch to ride around and see the country. You can pay 'em twice as much as you do the rest of us who do the work, but by hell, you can't make us drink with 'em."

"Why, you . . ." Harriman began.

"Shut up, Keno," Malloy snapped. He looked closely at Cotton as if seeing him in a new light. Then he nodded at the boss gunman. "If you have any differences, you'll settle them later. Much later. Savvy?"

Harriman put his flinty eyes on Cotton. He said, "You're the boss, Mr. Malloy, but I'm making one thing clear. This towheaded jigger with the fancy drinking ideas don't have to ride very far to get trouble if that's what he's looking for. When I settle with a man, I settle right. It's plumb permanent. With these." He patted the black-butted guns on his hips.

"Any day," Cotton murmured. It was a challenge Keno Harriman pretended not to hear.

"Take it easy," Santiam Jones said out of the corner of his mouth. "I've seen that jigger draw, and he ain't slow."

"Now that you're done arguing," Jackson Malloy said sharply, "I'll say what I came in here to say. We've got a visitor coming in on the stage. He's an important man, and I want him treated right." Malloy glanced at his watch. "The stage is due in about five minutes. I want every Broken Ring man down at the hotel when the stage rolls in."

"Who is this hombre?" Cotton asked.

"J. Francis Abernethy," Malloy said impressively. "Reckon you've all heard of the railroad man, Pierce Abernethy. This man is Pierce's brother. He'll stay at Broken Ring. Anything he wants that we can give him he gets." Malloy took one more look along the line of men in the manner of a man who expects to be obeyed without question. Then he wheeled out of the saloon.

"Five minutes," Cotton murmured. "I'm gonna push this, and we'll see what it gets us. Watch it, Santiam."

Keno Harriman had been cocked for trouble. Now apparently he thought Jackson Malloy's words had taken the edge off Cotton's temper, for he'd turned his back to the blond-headed buckaroo. Cotton came in close beside Harriman, and said so softly that the gunman barely heard, "Two graves in Luke Bray's yard. There's nothing lower than a woman killer, Keno."

Keno Harriman froze, his filled glass half lifted. Slowly he

BUCKAROO'S CODE 11

turned, and put his flinty eyes on Cotton. For just a moment fear was in them. Harriman had but one answer for all problems. The answer was simple—to kill the man who presents the problem. In that short interval the gunman made up his mind. He threw the whisky at Cotton's face while his other hand dipped for his gun.

Cotton Drennan had packed a good many smoky years into a short span of time. He understood men like Keno Harriman; he'd read the man's intent. When the gunman moved, Cotton ducked. The whisky sloshed over him as he came in with the speed of a striking panther. Harriman, trusting in guns, had not expected this maneuver. His fingers circled gun butt, but the Colt remained in leather. Cotton smashed a fist into the man's belly, driving the wind from him, and bringing him into a half-bend. Then Cotton raised his head suddenly, striking Harriman's chin hard.

The gunman went back, but he did not fall. One hand gripped the bar, and for a moment he swayed there uncertainly. Cotton heard Santiam Jones say, "Stand still, Ramsay." Cotton held back, waiting until Harriman's hand instinctively again dropped toward gun butt. Then Cotton sledged him on the jaw, knocked him away from the bar, and sent him into a spinning turn. Keno Harriman hit the floor, and lay still.

Cotton had time for a long look along the bar then. Santiam and Bill Curry had plucked guns and were covering Harriman's crew. Big-necked Butch Ramsay stood frozen, the hate that glittered in his beady eyes a wicked passion. Cotton grinned at him. "You boys ain't as tough as you figger you are, Butch. You oughta work for your living like we do."

"There'll be another day," Ramsay growled.

Beyond him Deuce Hinson mouthed an oath. "And I wanta be there when that day comes."

"We're leaving," Cotton said. "Don't get any ideas about shooting us in the back. The boss is figgering on us settling our troubles later." Then Cotton Drennan walked out, Santiam Jones and Bill Curry behind him. Harriman's gun crew watched them go without a word.

Curry took a deep breath when they were in the street. "I don't know what you're working on, Cotton, but you sure asked for a hunk of lead where it hurts when you busted Harriman that way."

Cotton smiled meagerly. "Bill, you saw how Harriman was. All he knows is to use a gun to kill. That's why Malloy's got that bunch here. Now just who is he after, and why?"

Curry cuffed back his Stetson and scratched his head. "There was a lot of nesters on this range when Malloy started Broken Ring, but they're mostly gone. Danged if I know why he's keeping 'em now. Do you?"

"No. It's too big an outfit just for the little fry that's left, which same being Fred Flagg."

"Fred's a little on the stubborn side," Santiam Jones said. "He'll stick."

"Like Luke Bray. No, it's hard to tell what sort of scheme Malloy's got cooking in his head, but I know one thing. The only way to lick men like Keno Harriman is to push 'em. I aim to keep 'em pushed. Mebbe we can save Fred Flagg's hide."

They were a half a block from the hotel when someone yelled, "Here she comes."

The stage rolled down the street, dust rising behind it and dripping from the wheels, and came to a stop in front of the hotel. A big crowd fanned out along the hotel porch and the sidewalk, with Jackson Malloy, the cigar still in his mouth, and his foreman, Red Donahue, in front.

Someone yelled, "Hurray for Abernethy." Another man yelled, "How about building a railroad for us up from the Columbia?"

J. Francis Abernethy was in no mood to talk about railroads when he stepped down from the stage. He was a younger man than Cotton expected, perhaps thirty, medium-tall and well built. His black suit was made gray by the dust upon it, and weariness showed itself on his square, arrogant face.

"We're mighty happy to have you here," Jackson Malloy was saying, shaking hands with Abernethy. "I've arranged for

BUCKAROO'S CODE

a room here in the hotel for you. You'll want to rest tonight, and tomorrow we'll ride out to Broken Ring. I'll expect you to stay there as my personal guest."

"Thank you, Mr. Malloy," Abernethy said, clipping his words precisely as he spoke. "That's very kind of you. Now the hotel room, if you don't mind."

Cotton did not say anything until Abernethy had gone into the hotel with Malloy and Red Donahue. Then he said thoughtfully, "Boys, something stinks, and it's got the smell of a lot of dollars."

"Meaning?" Santiam Jones asked.

"That Malloy is figgering on unloading Broken Ring on Mr. Abernethy for a big chunk of cash," Cotton said.

"But Broken Ring needs a watering place on White River," Santiam Jones pointed out. "Malloy couldn't get any big money until he's got a spot where cattle can get down to water."

"I know it," Cotton said, "and you know it. So does Bill here. Likewise Malloy. But does Mr. J. Francis Abernethy?"

"The spot's there," Curry said as if he had just made a great discovery. "Flagg's FF."

"Which may be too bad for Fred," Cotton said grimly. "That reminds me that I've got business with a lady. See you later, boys."

"He's sweet on that Flagg girl, ain't he?" Curry asked, looking at Cotton's ramrod-straight back as the buckaroo walked away.

"She's something to be sweet over," Santiam answered. "Now if I was twenty years younger . . ." He stopped, his eyes narrowing. "Bill, mebbe we'd better mosey down this alley. The view of the mountains from the other end of the alley is plumb entrancing."

"What in thunder . . ." Curry began as Jones took his arm and propelled him across the street.

"Keno Harriman and his bunch just came out of the Empress," Jones said, "and Keno looked plumb unhappy."

Chapter Two

Fired

JUNE FLAGG STEPPED OUT OF BEN HOWARD'S MERCANTILE, her arms full of packages, as Cotton came up. She stood for a time in the sharp mountain sunlight, smiling at Cotton, her dark blue eyes bright and friendly. A lovely, round-bodied girl, this June Flagg, who always made Cotton's breath come a little faster when he saw her. Nature had again demonstrated its sense of fitness in placing her here in this high and beautiful land of sky-piercing peaks. She was like a fine jewel dropped into an exquisite setting. These things were in Cotton's mind, but he was not a man who could put them into words. Instead he lifted his Stetson as he said, "Afternoon, June. I'll help you with those."

"Why, thanks, Cotton," the girl said. "I wondered if you were in town. Seems like I've seen all the Broken Ring men but you."

Cotton filled his arms with bundles, and walked beside June to the Flagg buckboard. Glancing sideways at her he asked,

BUCKAROO'S CODE 15

"Did you see the great man when he got out of the stage?"

"You mean Abernethy?"

"That's the gent. J. Francis Abernethy."

June nodded. "Dad and I were standing in front of the hotel. He wasn't the dude I thought he'd be. I'd say he was the kind of a man who could take care of himself in a fight."

"He looked all right," Cotton agreed. Apparently the girl had not thought how Abernethy's coming might affect her. "Is your dad around?"

"In the Palace, likely."

They had reached the buckboard, and Cotton put the girl's packages into it. For a moment he stood looking at her, stirred by her presence as he always was. He asked hesitantly, "Will you go to the dance with me tonight?"

It was a question, he thought, she had been afraid he would ask. She looked away quickly as if she didn't want to hurt him. "I'm sorry, Cotton. I told Mr. Malloy I'd go with him."

"June." He gripped her shoulders, and turned her so that she faced him. "Why?"

"It is my right," she said, suddenly defiant. "He's good-looking and he's nice. He's . . . he's . . ."

"He's got a pocketbook that's so full it squeals," Cotton finished savagely. "Is that it?"

"If it's any of your business, yes." Two little spots of red showed high on her cheeks. "I've watched Dad try to fight a living out of a homestead. I've watched my mother die helping. There must be something in life besides sweating and bleeding and breaking your heart."

Cotton had never heard June talk that way before. He'd always taken it for granted that she saw things the way he did. He had never told her he loved her, and now he was glad he hadn't. She had made her choice. Money was one thing he could not give her.

"There are other things about Jackson Malloy," Cotton said coldly, "that mebbe a woman can't see." He lifted his hat to her, and wheeled away.

16   WAYNE D. OVERHOLSER

Fred Flagg was in the Palace drinking with a group of small ranchers whose spreads lay north of Antioch along French Creek. He nodded at Cotton.

"How are you, son?" he asked.

"Fine as silk," Cotton answered. "I'd like to swap a little talk, Fred."

"Sure," Flagg said, and moved along the bar. "What's blowing up?"

"Trouble," Cotton answered. "I can smell it rolling in fast. Fred, has Malloy tried to buy you out?"

"Yeah," Flagg said, his round, sun-reddened face showing his surprise. "Why?"

Cotton laid his gaze on Flagg, and wondered how far he should go in telling the rancher what he suspected. Too, he wondered whether he should tell about the two graves on Luke Bray's place. Fred Flagg had little imagination. He was by nature a friendly man who held no hate, and he saw no reason why anybody should dislike him. Yet there was a stubborn quality about him. He could be pushed so far, and no farther. Like Luke Bray, he'd die on his FF before he'd get off unless it pleased him to move on.

"I was wondering," Cotton said slowly, "what sort of an offer he made."

"Fair enough," Flagg answered cautiously. "I just don't feel like moving. I won't bother Malloy's range none. It's easy enough to cross the river where my place is. I'll keep my beef on the west side."

Cotton saw that Flagg thought he was talking for Malloy. He said, "I'm drawing Broken Ring's pay right now, but it won't be much longer. If what I smell is right, I'll be rolling my soogans mighty damned quick."

"What are you trying to say, Cotton?" Flagg demanded.

"I'm saying that when Malloy decides to push you, you'll know you're pushed. Mebbe you didn't know it, but June's going to the dance with Malloy tonight. It don't add up, Fred. I reckon she'd never have any use for a thirty-a-month cowpoke like me, but I sure hate to see her going with a man like Jackson Malloy."

"So do I," Flagg said bitterly, "but June's got a head of her own. If she wants to go with Malloy, I sure can't stop her. Cotton, you've got something in your mind you ain't telling."

"Mebbe I'm smelling a mouse, but I think it's a rat. Malloy ain't a rancher. You know that. He's bought and sold a dozen places from here to the Rio Grande. Now mebbe he's ready to sell Broken Ring. What's he got without a watering place on the river, and where'd he get it except your FF?"

Flagg swore under his breath. "I'd never thought of it that way, but it sure adds up." Quick suspicion showed in his eyes as he stared at Cotton. "Are you trying to scare me into taking Malloy's offer? If you are, it sure ain't working, and you can go tell Malloy that."

"I'm not trying to do anything but make you see what's ahead," Cotton said wearily. "Why I stick my nose into other folks' business is sometimes a mystery to me, but I seem to keep on doing it. Now you can do as you damned please, Fred. If you want to hang tight and get a dose of hot lead, it's your business. Only you've got June to think of besides your own stubborn hide."

Cotton wheeled out of the saloon, the momentary satisfaction that had been in him a few hours before when he'd stood between Santiam Jones and Bill Curry in the Empress completely burned away. There would be no fun going to the dance when Jackson Malloy was taking June. He'd provoked a fight with Keno Harriman, and he thought savagely, as he strode down the street, that he'd have felt better to have let it go to gunplay. Now he'd tried to help Fred Flagg, and all he'd got out of it was the feeling on Flagg's part that he was trying to work a slick one for Jackson Malloy. There was nothing left but the steak he'd promised himself at Big Nose Charlie's, and a good drunk with Santiam and Bill. He'd likely wind up in Antioch jail, but it would be fun while it lasted. There would

18   WAYNE D. OVERHOLSER

be some broken noses, and he hoped one of them would belong
to the Broken Ring ramrod, Red Donahue.

Cotton found Santiam Jones and Bill Curry in the stable at
the north end of Main Street. "I've been hearing my tapeworm
holler for the last half hour. Let's mosey over to Charlie's, and
feed it."

Jones rubbed a hand over his lean jaw, and stared at Cotton
speculatively. He said, "Son, we've been watching some queer
things from here, like Malloy and Donahue taking Abernethy
into the hotel dining room."

"Nothing funny about that."

"No," Santiam was watching Cotton's face, "but Malloy had
June Flagg with him."

Cotton swore softly. "I can't do anything about it. I wish
I'd stayed out in the sagebrush. Anybody who tries to figger
women out are sure building themselves up for a headache."

"Now one more little item," Santiam said lazily. "Bill and
me took a walk when we seen Keno and his outfit come out
of the Empress. Reckon Keno was looking for Donahue. He
sure looked proddy, Keno did. Well sir, me and Bill circled
through the alley, and came back on Jefferson Street. We'd
fiddled away some time, figgering mebbe Keno would be back
in the Empress. Well, he wasn't. He had his outfit on the street
corner, and Keno was mad as a bull with a hornet sitting on
his tail. He was cussing you, and he was cussing Malloy. You
know why, Cotton?"

"I'm no mind reader," Cotton snapped.

"Son, you wouldn't have believed yourself if you had been.
Keno was cussing Malloy because the boss said Keno was
gonna let you alone. If you showed up with a slug in your
brisket, Keno and his whole bunch got fired. Now, what do
you think of that?"

"I think somebody's crazy."

"It sure ain't me," Santiam grunted. "Me and Bill listened
to that much, and then we ambled back the way we'd come.
We didn't hear nothing about Malloy saying to lay off us. With

BUCKAROO'S CODE

Keno feeling like he is, it'd be like him to start smoking his hogleg the minute he saw us."

"Let's go eat in the dining room," Cotton said suddenly.

"I thought you said Charlie's," Bill Curry objected. "Charlie always has better steaks . . ."

"I want to try the dining room," Cotton said. "I'd just about decided it was time I stopped doing favors for other people, and likewise time we lit a shuck out of here. Now I reckon I'll stick around long enough to find out why Jackson Malloy would want to keep Keno from plugging me."

Cotton picked out a table along the side wall in the hotel dining room, and took the chair that gave him a view of the front of the room. Malloy, Donahue, Abernethy, and June Flagg had a table near the windows. Cotton was too far away to hear the talk, but he could see they were enjoying themselves. June was wearing a white dress; Cotton had never seen her prettier, nor had he ever heard her laugh more than she was laughing now.

Cotton saw the blond girl who was sitting alone near the door into the lobby, and paid no more attention to her. He watched June rise, and take Abernethy's arm as they moved toward the lobby. He heard Abernethy say in his precise way, "I can't believe that there could be anyone as lovely as you in this wild country."

Malloy was the last of the four to leave the dining room. The blond girl near the door looked up just as Malloy passed her table. The Broken Ring owner stopped dead still, and stared down at the girl. She met his eyes, and held them until he turned suddenly and walked away hurriedly as if trying to leave a distasteful memory behind him.

"More funny business," Santiam said. "Who is the gal, Cotton?"

"Never saw her before," Cotton answered, "but if I'm guessing right, we'll see more of her."

"They don't know how to cook steak here," Bill Curry said in an aggrieved tone. "This here's tougher'n a boot heel. Even ketchup don't make it good. Hod dang it, Cotton, why didn't we eat at Charlie's? Now, that boy can sure cook a steak."

"Get your mind off your belly for a while," Cotton advised. "We've got more important things to worry about. Now, take that girl. Her hair's the color of wheat when it's dead ripe."

"Why don't you take her to the dance?" Santiam asked.

"It's a good idea," Cotton agreed.

Cotton was finishing his pie when Red Donahue walked in from the lobby, pulled up a chair, and sat down. "Cotton," he demanded sourly, "what was this ruckus with Keno about?"

Cotton put his fork down, and looked at the Broken Ring ramrod. Donahue's hair was copper-colored, his eyes were green and were set too closely together. He was as big as Jackson Malloy, but the two men were not at all alike. Where the owner was a direct man, the foreman was shrewd and cunning, and in him was a cruel streak that Cotton had seen many times. Now Donahue sat slouched in his chair, apparently at ease, but Cotton knew the man too well to be caught off guard.

"I don't like gunhands," Cotton said bluntly. "I've been working for Broken Ring almost a year now. All that time you've had Keno Harriman and his gunslicks on the pay roll. Malloy pays 'em twice what he does us," he nodded at Bill Curry and Santiam Jones, "and all they do is ride around through the junipers. It just don't set with me, Red."

"So it don't set with you," Donahue said mockingly. "There's one thing you can do, feller."

"It might be a good deal for you and your bully boys," Cotton said softly, "if I pulled out, seeing as I know something you wouldn't like to get out. Them graves had brush on them. If I hadn't dug around a little I wouldn't have found 'em."

"Some men see too much, and die young," Donahue said lazily. He straightened up, and brought his chair closer to the table. "Cotton, how much is it worth for you to leave the country?"

BUCKAROO'S CODE

Cotton saw the play coming. He'd dropped his hands to his sides. Now he lifted a gun from holster, but kept it under the table top. "I wouldn't leave for all the dinero you can get your hands on, hombre," he said, and waited until he saw a slight movement of Donahue's right shoulder. There was the ominous sound of a gun being cocked as he added, "Let that iron slide back. Put your hands on the table, Red. You must be kind o' scary to try that. Mebbe I'd be smart if I let you have it."

Red Donahue froze. Slowly he brought his hands out from under the edge of the table and laid them palm down on the top. "I've pegged you a little low, Cotton. You're tougher than I figgered. First you knock Keno colder'n a froze beef, and then you get the jump on me. Mebbe I've put my money on the wrong man." He looked at Santiam Jones, and then at fat Bill Curry. "These boys kind o' play with you, don't they, Cotton? Well, there's only one answer. You're fired, all three of you."

"In other words," Cotton said, "you don't want anybody working for Broken Ring that's got ears to hear and eyes to see with. I reckon that's all right with us, ain't it, boys?"

"Sure is," Santiam Jones said. "I was getting danged tired looking at Red's ugly face."

"Same here," Bill Curry agreed.

"No hurry," Donahue said. "You can get your time tomorrow."

"There's just one thing I want to settle, Red," Cotton said. He rose and came around to where Donahue sat. "I've always wondered," he brought a fist up in a cruel blow that caught Donahue squarely on the jaw and knocked him out of his chair, "if you had a glass jaw." Donahue didn't answer. He was out cold. "Yep, he sure does." Cotton moved back to his chair and sat down. "Soon as I finish this pie we'll be moving."

"Yeah," Santiam Jones said gloomily, staring at Donahue's still figure, "mebbe we should have moved sooner. About yesterday. You sure are good at hunting for trouble, and finding it."

Chapter Three

Gun Trap

THE BLOND GIRL HAS WATCHED THE SCENE BETWEEN COTTON and Red Donahue with close interest. She was waiting in the lobby when Cotton and his friends left the dining room. Cotton caught her eye, felt her invitation, and moved to where she stood.

"I reckon you're new in Antioch, ma'am," Cotton said, holding his Stetson in his hand.

"Yes," the girl said. "I came in on the stage yesterday."

"I thought . . . I mean . . . if you're new in town . . ." Cotton stammered. He swallowed, and blurted, "Mebbe you'd like to go to the dance tonight?"

"No, I wouldn't," the girl answered, "but wait." She caught Cotton's arm as he started to turn. "I think you're the man I'm looking for."

Cotton knew he had never seen her before in his life. She was the kind of woman a man, having once seen, would never forget. She was small, almost doll-like in size and in the perfection of her features, but there was a straight-backed pride about her and a sharp determination showing in her oval face that indicated size was no measure of her strength. About her was something which said clearly enough that life had taught her the fullness of human emotions, that she knew both how to love and to hate.

"I don't reckon you're looking for me, ma'am," Cotton said,"seeing as we never saw each other before. Sorry I asked you about the dance. I just thought . . . "

"That's all right, Mr. . . . ?" She was still holding his arm, looking him over from his white-haired head to his booted feet.

"They just call me Cotton, Miss . . ."

"Taney. Sandra. You can call me that, Cotton. I think we'll get along." She let his arm go now, and stepped back, head cocked a little as she studied him. For a time her blue eyes rested on his holstered gun. Suddenly she nodded as if her mind was made up. "Yes, we'll get along."

"I feel a little bit like a prize bull in a stock show," Cotton drawled. "I don't reckon I'm any prize."

"I'm sorry." Her smile cut away the grim determination from her face. "You see, I want a man to do a very important job. You aren't working, are you?"

"For Broken Ring," Cotton said.

"That's Jackson Malloy's outfit, isn't it?"

"Yes."

"Wasn't it Malloy's foreman you just knocked out?"

"Yes."

"I understood him to say you were fired. Now I'm . . ."

"Mebbe Red figgers I'm fired," Cotton said easily, "but I ain't quite ready to quit. There's a few things simmering on the fire that kind o' interest me. I reckon I'll have a talk with Malloy."

"But I have money," Sandra Taney insisted. "I'll pay you two hundred dollars a month. It might be a permanent arrangement that would suit both of us."

"Two hundred dollars a month?" Cotton scratched his head. "Listen, lady. For that kind of money you'd expect me to rob a railroad, which same ain't in my line."

"No robbing of railroads," Sandra said quickly. "It's really quite simple. All I want now is for you to marry me."

"What?" There was a strange sinking feeling in Cotton's stomach. "I reckon I didn't hear that right."

"Yes, you heard me," Sandra Taney said composedly. "I'll pay you to marry me. We will either homestead here, or, if Malloy takes you back, I'll live with you on Broken Ring."

"Pleased to have met you, ma'am." Cotton nodded, and started to move away.

"Wait." There was a strained note in the girl's voice. "Am I as bad-looking as that? It might not be for long. I have one definite thing to do. I need you. How much money . . ."

"Ma'am," Cotton said softly, "I've met up with some queer things, but nothing like this before. You ain't bad-looking by no manner of means, and I don't give a dog-gone how long it would last. There's only one thing I aim to stay clear of. That's getting hobbles put on me with a pocketful of dinero. So long."

Cotton didn't look back, but he knew she was standing there, staring after him, and he had a feeling that she was close to tears. To have brought tears from a self-possessed woman like Sandra Taney would have been close to performing a major miracle, and Cotton wondered what had brought her to this position where she had tried to buy a husband, and what lay between her and Malloy.

Outside, Santiam Jones leaned a bony shoulder against a porch post, and stood staring into the gathering dusk, a half-smoked cigarette dangling from his lips, the smoke drifting across his weather-scarred face. "You get the gal roped and tied?" he asked when Cotton came up beside him.

"I had her tied all right," Cotton grunted, "but I let her up, and ran. Where's Bill?"

"He went down to the Empress to get some cigars. Cotton, no use of us hanging around this burg. Over in the Harney valley there's some big outfits. I'd like to see what it looks like over there."

BUCKAROO'S CODE   25

Cotton grinned sourly as he shaped up a smoke. "I'm getting myself into a hell of a fix, but I'm not hitting out for the Harney valley country yet. What's happened now?"

Santiam tossed his cigarette into the street. "Cotton, I've been in spots like this before. I've traveled the road twice as long as you have. I can see what's coming, and I tell you it's time to get out. There ain't a damned thing to keep any of the three of us here. If we stay, it'd be just like sitting on a rock pile during a thunderstorm, and telling lightning to take a crack at us."

Cotton thumbed a match to life, and held the flame to his cigarette. In the year that he'd known Santiam Jones he'd learned to respect the man's cool and sober judgment. Santiam was often gruff and sour, but when the chips were down, he was a man to ride the river with. So Cotton waited.

Presently Jones said, "She builds up a little different each time. The pattern mebbe ain't quite the same, but it'll roll out till it looks like the rest. You've got gunslingers like Keno Harriman who don't live by no standard except whatever it takes to earn their pay. Red Donahue is about the same size, but he's a little smarter, and he'll have his nest feathered when Keno is swamping out a saloon if he lives that long. Jackson Malloy don't want nothing but money. Now look at it any way you want to, and where do you fit? On the receiving end of a .45 slug. Son, I tell you it's time to move."

Still Cotton said nothing. Santiam stared at him from under shaggy brows. "All right," he said heavily. "There's one more item. So far you haven't run up against this Abernethy hombre. I've got my doubts that this jigger is the J. Francis Abernethy he claims he is. He don't look like no Eastern dude to me. Anyhow, June just left with him. They was walking down the street toward the courthouse the last I saw of 'em."

"All right." Cotton flipped his cigarette into the street. "A man can't do no more than try. Mr. J. Francis Abernethy has more dinero than Jackson Malloy. June can do her shopping. Me, I'm broke and out of a job. Let's have another drink, and light a shuck out of town."

Bill Curry was having a drink with Al Rhyman, another Broken Ring hand, when Cotton and Santiam came in. Cotton stood beside them for a time, then drifted back to a table and sat in on a poker game. There was no fun in it. The taste of it was like lukewarm coffee watered thin.

Presently Cotton left the table, moved along the street to the end of the board walk, and came back. For want of anything else to do he climbed the stairs to the lodge hall above Ben Howard's Mercantile. He shouldered his way through the men in the hall and doorway, passed within five feet of Keno Harriman and Butch Ramsay, and moved on to a vacant spot against the wall.

Abernethy was dancing with June. It was, except for the brief moment in front of the hotel, Cotton's first chance to see the Easterner. His high-boned face held a dark coat of tan. He had changed into a blue serge suit, and as he and June danced by Cotton noted how the man's thick shoulders made a tight fit in his coat. Later, when the dance had stopped, and Cotton made his way toward them, June saw him and smiled her invitation to him.

"I wondered why you weren't here," June said.

"There is only one answer," Cotton said distantly, "which you know."

"But there was a blonde," June murmured.

"An observing woman," Cotton said.

Abernethy was listening, puzzlement showing in his broad face. Cotton winked, and held out his hand when June said, "Mr. Abernethy, meet Cotton Drennan from Broken Ring."

"Folks just call me Cotton."

Abernethy scowled. "I hope I'll merit a name out here like Cotton. 'J. Francis Abernethy' sounds as if I'd come out of the social register, and a man's pedigree doesn't mean anything in Oregon. In fact, it shouldn't anywhere."

BUCKAROO'S CODE 27

"Somebody will think of a name," Cotton said. "Mebbe you'll like it and mebbe you won't, but if you get stuck with it, you're stuck. Are you buying a spread out here?"

"I have hopes," Abernethy answered, "if I find what I like. I don't care to make money. I have all I need. I want a place where I can fish and hunt." He gestured wearily. "I hope, however, I can build up a good ranch. There is far more satisfaction in accomplishing some worthwhile thing than merely counting the number of dollars you may have in the bank."

"Perhaps you're right," Cotton said, giving June a straight look. "I've accomplished quite a bit today, but I sure don't have much trouble counting my dollars." He nodded at Abernethy. "Glad to have met you. I hope if we meet again we will be on the same side." He moved away, and when he reached for the door, he looked back. Abernethy, deeply puzzled, was staring after him.

Jackson Malloy was not in the hall. Red Donahue was, but he carefully avoided looking at Cotton. Keno Harriman and Butch Ramsay were gone. These things Cotton noted as he left the lodge hall. He paused on the board walk, thinking he would find Santiam and Bill, and tell them he was ready to hit leather. There was nothing else, he felt, in Antioch or on White River range that made his staying longer worth while. He'd drifted since he was a kid. He had stayed here longer than he had ever stayed anywhere else since he'd left home. Now a great bitterness came into him when he thought how much his staying had been because of June Flagg.

All of these things folded in together, a strange and fantastic pattern that was not yet clear. Why was Sandra Taney here, and why was she willing to pay a strange man to marry her? Why, too, had Malloy acted in such a peculiar manner when he'd seen her? And why was Malloy paying fighting wages to Keno Harriman and his gun crew? Cotton moved along the walk to the bank, and stopping to smoke a cigarette, thought of these things. The rest of it was clear enough. Somehow Malloy had been able to use June to bait Abernethy. Broken Ring would get its watering place at Flagg's FF. Malloy would take his money, and move on to do it all over again somewhere else.

It was fair, Cotton told himself. June could marry Abernethy, and have what she wanted. Perhaps she'd stay on Broken Ring. Or perhaps she'd go with Abernethy back to New York. If money could buy the things June cared for, it was all right. She'd be happy, J. Francis Abernethy would be a lucky man, and Fred Flagg would be safe enough with his FF a part of Broken Ring.

Then Cotton remembered the ashes of Luke Bray's cabin, and the two graves that had been covered. Any casual passerby would think the cabin had burned accidentally, that Luke Bray and his wife had left their homestead as many others had done out there in the desert. Only Cotton knew better. He'd stopped and eaten with them many times. He knew the plans they had, the sweat and labor and pain the homestead had cost them. No, the only way Luke Bray could have been taken off Broken Ring range was by a murderer's bullet, and that was exactly what had happened.

Cotton tossed away his cigarette stub. Still he didn't move, for another thought had come to him. He had assumed that Malloy had ordered the murder of Luke Bray and his wife, but Malloy, unless Cotton was entirely mistaken in his judgment of the man, was not a killer. There was no real reason for the Brays to be killed. It wasn't a case like Flagg's FF. Sand Spring was not big. It would be valuable only for a man who aimed to run a small outfit, and that was exactly what Bray had planned. There must, then, be some other reason for the murder of Luke Bray and his wife.

A man was coming along the sidewalk toward Cotton. As he passed the lighted windows of the Palace Saloon, Cotton saw that it was Jackson Malloy. It was possible that Malloy had nothing to do with the Brays' murder. It was possible, too, that he didn't know about it. This would be as good a time as any to find out, Cotton thought, and stepped away from the bank to stop Malloy. In that moment a gun boomed from across the street. The heavy thunder of the gun rolled the length of the street. Before the echo died, Cotton's gun was in his hand and driving lead into the alley mouth from which the shot had come.

Men boiled out of the Palace and the Empress and the other saloons along the street. Twice Cotton fired; then raced across the dust strip, gun palmed. He heard someone behind him shout, "It's Malloy." Farther down the street another gun spoke. Cotton felt the breath of the slug upon his cheek, and went on. Once more the second killer squeezed trigger, but Cotton had reached the opposite sidewalk by then. He crossed, went on into the alley, and slipped around the rear corner of the Empress. No one was in the alley, or if anyone was, he had taken refuge in the piles of rubbish that cluttered the alley.

There was one way to find out, Cotton thought. He stepped into the alley so that he could be seen, and quickly ducked back. No shot greeted his appearance. The ambusher must have gone into the Empress through the back door. Cotton followed that path, and saw that the only man in the saloon was Keno Harriman. He stood against the bar, leaning hard as if the strength had gone from his legs. He lifted his eyes to Cotton, and appeared not to see him.

Cotton moved around Harriman, and waited. Presently Butch Ramsay came in through the back, and went up to Harriman. He poured himself a drink, and said something. It was apparent to Cotton that Keno Harriman was not at all drunk. A moment later the barkeep came in with the flow from the street. He said, "If that slug had been an inch lower, Malloy would be a dead pigeon right now."

Ben Howard, the storekeeper, saw Cotton, and asked, "Did you find anybody in the alley, Cotton?"

"No. I reckon I got there too late. Didn't hit anybody, either."

Dib Alcott, the town marshal, heard what Cotton said.

"I wondered who it was that cut loose at the damned drygulcher," Alcott said. "Of course it ain't murder, but it could have been easy as not. I don't know anybody who would want to kill Jack Malloy. I always figgered he had a lot of friends."

"All of us have our enemies," Cotton murmured, his eyes on Harriman. The gunman had straightened now, and turned, all pretense of drunkenness gone. Red Donahue had come in, and was standing inside the batwings, his green eyes bright with desire to kill.

"Well, I'll be getting me a lantern," Alcott said, "and having a look in the alley, but I don't reckon I'll find anything."

Men went back to tables and took up their cards again. Some stayed at the bar. Ramsay had drifted across to a side window where he stayed, apparently watching a card game, but as watchful as a panther ready to spring. Cotton saw that, and he saw a fourth man, Deuce Hinson, standing behind Donahue.

Cotton recognized this exactly for what it was, a gun trap ready to be sprung on him any minute, and Donahue would be the man to give the word to spring it. Either the Broken Ring ramrod or Keno Harriman would gladly pull a trigger on him. They knew that he knew about the killing of Luke Bray and his wife. The chances were they knew he had a good guess who had shot Malloy. There was only one way for Cotton to play this: the hard way. That was exactly what he did. He turned to the barkeep, and asked in a tone loud enough for Red Donahue to hear, "Was Harriman in here before Malloy was shot?"

"No, he wasn't," the barkeep said.

Cotton nodded as if he had known it all the time. He made a quick turnabout, and moved directly toward Red Donahue.

Chapter Four

A New Ramrod
For Broken Ring

FROM WATCHING RED DONAHUE WORK HIS HORSES AND CREW, Cotton knew that as long as the ramrod had the upper hand, he was utterly ruthless and wicked, but there was a breaking point in him. Stripped of the veneer of apparent toughness, he was a man of no great courage. Now, as Cotton bore down upon him, a doubt showed in his cat-green eyes as his hand went up to his face to touch the dark bruise Cotton's fist had given him in the hotel dining room.

"Think fast, Red," Cotton said as he came on. "If you call it tough, I'll put a bullet into your guts. Is this a good night to die, Donahue?"

Donahue made no answer. He stood there, fear breaking across his face, trying to hold his position, and showing, by the quick shake of the head he gave Keno Harriman, that he wasn't man enough to do it.

"Stand aside, Red," Cotton said, and went on squarely at Donahue.

One step separated them. Donahue held his place that long,

then his eyes wavered from Cotton's, and he moved over toward Deuce Hinson. There he stood as Cotton went out.

A grim smile touched Cotton's lips as he walked toward the Palace Saloon. Twice in one night he had come out ahead of Red Donahue. Donahue, in his scheming, crafty way, would not let that go. If Cotton left Broken Ring at this time, it would look like a showing of fear. It had become a personal matter now between him on one side and Donahue and Harriman on the other. Before Malloy's shooting, Cotton had been ready to leave White River range. Now he could not go. Santiam Jones would not understand. He would say pride was a danged fool thing to get a man killed over, and that the fight was still none of Cotton's business, he'd be well out of it.

So Cotton looked in the Palace for Santiam Jones and Bill Curry. He wanted to tell them that somewhere along the line the thing had changed. He couldn't tell them exactly how or where. Or perhaps there had been no change. Perhaps he was seeing it straight now. The death of Luke Bray and his wife hadn't changed. It was inevitable that Red Donahue and Keno Harriman, knowing what Cotton knew, would attempt to kill him. This time Donahue's nerve had broken. Another time would be different. Perhaps an attempt to get him from ambush, as they had tried to get Malloy.

Neither Santiam nor Bill Curry was in the Palace. As Cotton left the saloon to try the Lucky Chance he met Al Rhyman.

"The boss wants to see you, Cotton," Rhyman said. "He's in his hotel room."

"Is he hurt bad?" Cotton asked, turning toward the hotel with Rhyman.

"Reckon he won't have nothing more'n a headache," Rhyman growled, "but if that slug had been any lower, Broken Ring wouldn't have no owner." The little buckaroo looked at Cotton sharply. "Who do you reckon did that shooting?"

"I couldn't be sure," Cotton answered.

"There's sure some funny things going on around here," Rhyman said, "that I don't understand. I never liked Keno

BUCKAROO'S CODE   33

Harriman and his bunch no more than you and Santiam did, but I reckon I never had the guts to bust 'em like you did today. What started it, Cotton?"

"I don't know that exactly," Cotton returned, "but I pushed Keno a little in the Empress, and I've had to keep on pushing ever since."

Rhyman didn't say anything more until they had crossed the hotel lobby and climbed the stairs to Malloy's room. Then Rhyman said, "Go on in, Cotton. I'll stick around out here. Bud's in the room down the hall," Rhyman jerked a thumb toward the door, "getting some sleep. After a while I'll boost him out and he can play guard."

Cotton nodded, turned the knob, and slid into the room. Malloy lay propped up in bed, a bandage around his head, the inevitable cigar in his mouth. A chair had been pulled up to the bed. On the seat were cigars, matches, and a .45. A low-burning lamp stood on the bureau. The shade had been pulled.

"Howdy, Cotton," Malloy said, motioning toward the foot of the bed. "Sit down."

Cotton tossed his Stetson on the bed, and sat down. "Heard you wanted to see me," he said. "Before you get lined out, mebbe I'd better tell you Red fired me this evening."

"I know." Malloy nodded. "We'll talk about that later." He gave Cotton a close look. "You know who took a shot at me?"

"I ain't sure," Cotton answered. For the first time in the year he'd been on Broken Ring, Cotton saw Jackson Malloy as a man who was not sure of himself. It showed in the way his eyes shifted around the room, the nervous manner of tonguing his cigar from one side of his mouth to the other.

"You've got a hunch?" Malloy said.

Cotton shrugged. "I ain't sure," he repeated.

"They tell me you were on the street," Malloy said, "when the killer cut loose. You shot back, and ran across the street after him. Then another man down the street opened up on you. Now I never thought you had any great affection for me. I reckon nobody does." He jerked the cigar from his mouth and slammed it into the spittoon. He tried to grin, but it was a sour attempt. "I don't know what's happened to me, Cotton. Reckon I've tried too hard to make money, and I'm getting what I had coming. What I want to know is, why did you pitch into the scrap?"

"It ain't a scrap when a sneaky killer stands in an alley," Cotton answered, "and shoots a man down in the street. That kind of coyote needs killing, and I tried to do the chore."

Malloy thought that over. He picked up a fresh cigar, and studied it as he rolled it between his fingers. He said, "You've been working for me almost a year. You're a good man. Even Red says that, but you haven't stood out much, one way or the other. You did your work, and you earned your pay. Now for some reason you go off the deep end, and you've got yourself into a fix where Harriman or Donahue or both of them will try to kill you. What happened?"

"They've already tried," Cotton said.

"Did you get either one of them?" Malloy asked in quick interest.

Cotton shook his head. "Donahue caved. They had me dead to rights, four of 'em set up in the Empress, but Donahue decided it wasn't the right night to die."

Malloy's face showed his disappointment. "You still haven't told me what happened."

"Instead I'll ask you a question. Did you know Luke Bray and his wife had been killed, their cabin burned, and they were buried in the yard with some brush thrown over the dirt so the graves wouldn't be seen?"

"No." Malloy's face showed his surprise. "Who did it?"

"I ain't sure of that, either," Cotton answered. "I don't like to accuse a man of murder until I am sure, but I know this: Donahue had warned Luke to pull stakes, saying that you were clearing all the nesters off your range. Luke was a stubborn cuss, so he stayed. Santiam and Bill were camped by Bridger

BUCKAROO'S CODE   35

Butte, and Keno Harriman's gang rode by a few days before I found Bray's cabin burned."

Malloy cursed. "I didn't give any order like that to Red. Bray wasn't hurting me. I've shoved a lot of nesters off my range since I've been here. Some of them I bought out; some I chased. Donahue did it, and I'm sorry to say there was one or two killings, but I didn't aim to bother Bray. We don't need the range in the desert."

"I'm not sure what got into me today," Cotton said thoughtfully. He drew tobacco and paper from his pocket, built a smoke, and touched a match to it. "My folks were nesters in Montana. My dad was shot by a range hog. We had to leave, and Ma died a year later. I've been making out by myself since I was twelve. Luke seemed a lot like my dad. Him and his wife had a lot of hard luck, but it looked like they were going to make out all right. Now they're dead. I guess that's what happened to me. It's no good trying to get the sheriff down from the county seat. He couldn't prove nothing. Besides, it's a hell of a long ways, and chances are he wouldn't come. Mebbe I'd better take care of it myself."

"You may have some help," Malloy said soberly. "From what you said in the Empress this afternoon I figured there was something else biting you."

"I said what I had to say about it then," Cotton said. "Now mebbe you can tell me why you've been paying fighting wages to gunhawks like Harriman's crew when you didn't need them at all."

"It's like getting a ton boulder strapped on your neck," Malloy growled, "and not being able to get it off. I couldn't fire Donahue, so he's been sitting in the driver's seat. Harriman was his idea, and Harriman takes his orders. I just pay the wages."

"What does Donahue want?"

"If it was Harriman or some of his men who tried to kill me," Malloy answered, "I'd say Red wants Broken Ring." Malloy struck a match on the wall, and lighted his cigar.

"Cotton, that's why I wanted to talk to you. I buy to sell. You know that. I never did intend to run Broken Ring. I came to Antioch two years ago to look around. Nobody lived on Broken Ring range but nesters. I built a big house for bait, brought in some beef so it would look good, and threw out my lines. Abernethy is the answer. If he likes Broken Ring, he'll buy it." Malloy took his cigar out of his mouth. "I'm asking one hundred thousand dollars for the spread, which is small change to a man like Abernethy."

Cotton tossed his cigarette stub into the spittoon. "I wouldn't know about that," he said dryly, and thought about June Flagg.

"The thing is that Red has apparently decided to move in," Malloy went on. "Either I lose everything I've got, or I fight. I know I've got some good buckaroos, and if I could do it over I'd have fought it out with Red before. Al Rhyman is as loyal as they come. So are Bud Kroft, Santiam, Bill Curry, and the rest. Perhaps I don't get any love from them, but I think they're loyal."

Cotton nodded, and said nothing. Malloy was watching him intently. He said, "They're good men, and they don't like Red. They would have respected me more if I'd fired Red months ago. Now I've got to. When Red goes, I'll need a ramrod, and I'm offering you the job. I think Abernethy will buy Broken Ring. He'll make a big spread out of it, and you'll have a good job."

Still Cotton said nothing, and still he was thinking of June Flagg. Or June Abernethy she might be then. It would be a strange prank of fate to give him the ramrod job on a spread of which she was the mistress.

"Well?" Malloy asked. "Is it a deal?"

"It's a deal," Cotton said. "I reckon I wouldn't want to work for no pilgrim like Abernethy, but that'll wait." He picked up his Stetson. "I'm wondering about June. She told me you were taking her to the dance, but it looked like Abernethy to me."

Malloy's face reddened. "I . . . I—well, I invited her to have supper with us, and Abernethy seemed to think she was something special, so I suggested he take her. I didn't know there was anything between you and June."

"There isn't," Cotton said quickly, "only it struck me as queer. I was curious about something else. You remember the blond girl in the dining room tonight?"

Malloy's molars took a fresh and vicious grip on his cigar. "We'll not discuss her. Now there's one chore you'll have to do tonight, Cotton. I've got every reason in the world to respect June. I've asked her to marry me, but she won't have me." He gestured wearily. "Looks as if my sins have finally caught up with me. The one woman I want above everything else says no."

Cotton stood motionless beside the bed watching Malloy. The man was staring across the room at nothing at all, seeing, Cotton thought, a past he would like to forget.

"I started from nothing," Malloy went on finally, "and now I'll ride out of White River range with one hundred thousand dollars in my pocket, only June won't be riding with me." Malloy's eyes snapped back to Cotton's face. "I told you there was one more chore. I reckon the dance is over. Haven't heard the music for quite a spell. June was going home with her dad. I want you to ride to the FF. You'll get there about as soon as they will. Tell them I've got to have the FF, and I'll give anything within reason. Tell Fred to set his own price."

"And if Fred won't take it?"

"He's got to. Tomorrow when we get back to Broken Ring, I'll get all hands together. I'll fire Red and Harriman's bunch, and I'll tell them you're the boss from here on out. It'll be touch and go for a minute, but I don't think Red is the kind who'll jump me in the open. I think they'll get off Broken Ring without any trouble. Now my way of getting at folks isn't what happened to Luke Bray, but if Red gets the bit in his teeth, he won't stop at nothing. Whatever happens, I don't want June hurt. Tell them that, Cotton."

"I will," Cotton said. He moved to the door, and paused, his hand on the knob.

"Get moving," Malloy said irritably. "There's no telling what Red is up to."

Still Cotton did not move. He pinned his gaze on Malloy, and said, "It looks to me like you're in a hell of a tight, Malloy. Ever since you've been here you've had Harriman and his lead tossers around, using 'em when you had to get tough with some nester who was a little more stubborn than the rest. Now they're turning on you like a pack of wolves turn on one of their own bunch when he goes down. You've got to fight, and you're aiming to use the buckaroos who have been doing the work and getting half the wages. You know I've held up my end today, and so you figger I'm the one who might have a chance to pull you through. That right?"

"Yeah," Malloy admitted reluctantly. "You take the hide off and leave it looking pretty bald, but that's about the size of it."

"All right. Now there's one thing you ain't made yourself clear on, and before I get into this any farther, I'm gonna know the answer. Why have you kept Harriman's bunch on Broken Ring?"

"I told you," Malloy said hotly. "I said—"

"Yeah, I know," Cotton broke in. "I know what you said. You claimed you couldn't fire Donahue. I want the why to that."

"It is none of your business," Malloy said, anger narrowing his eyes.

"All right," Cotton nodded somberly. "Then I reckon I don't want that job we was talking about. I'll get my stuff, and I'll be riding on."

Cotton had the door half open before Malloy spoke. "Come back in here, and shut the door." When Cotton had complied, Malloy demanded, "Why is it so important that you know?"

"When I take this ramrod job," Cotton answered, "I'm into trouble up to my neck. I don't want no deuces running wild. I want to know all the answers before it's too late."

For a moment Malloy rubbed the square width of his chin

BUCKAROO'S CODE   39

as he stared thoughtfully at Cotton. Then he said, "You don't
leave me much choice, Cotton. I'm hoping you will keep this
between us, because it would sure play hell with me if it got
out. As far as I know, Donahue has kept mum. I had some
trouble in Arizona. The sheriff called it murder, and I'll admit
the evidence was against me. Donahue helped me bust out. I'd
have been better off to have stayed, and stood trial. Now if I
don't give Donahue what he wants, he swears he'll turn me
in. If I went back now, my running out the first time would be
against me, and I'd sure get a rope halter quick and sudden."

"I see." Still Cotton didn't move. He thought back over
what had been happening. "Then Harriman and his crowd stay
on because Donahue's blackmailing you? And Donahue knew
about your scheme to sell to Abernethy?"

"He knew all right," Malloy said grimly. "I was to give him
a split, and he was to let me alone. He's stuck to me like a
leech ever since we got out of Arizona. He's a tricky son, and
it looks now like he's playing his own game all the way. We
needed Harriman's outfit at first to clear the range. We don't
now, and Donahue never has said exactly why he wants 'em
kept. Looks like all the time he was figuring on cutting my
throat when the sign was right."

"How do you figger you'll get rid of Donahue tomorrow?
And how did you make it stick with Harriman when he was
going to plug me today, and you said you'd fire him if I turned
up dead?"

"The answer to the last question is that I'm boss as far as
Harriman knows. At least Donahue wasn't supposed to say
anything else. As to the first question, I don't see a way out
as long as Donahue's alive." He gestured wearily. "I am not
a killer, but after the years I've jumped whenever Donahue
opened his mug, I'm ready to do anything to free myself. Now
will you slope out of here?"

"Yes," Cotton said. He stepped into the hall, closing the
door behind him. Al Rhyman was still there. "I thought mebbe
you was purty well spooked, Al, but things are stacking up a

little different than I thought. You may have fireworks before morning."

"We'll be ready," Rhyman said.

It was after midnight when Cotton left the hotel. He slid through the door and stood quietly against the wall for a time, eyes searching the darkness of the street for a shadow that might be a man's. The gloom of the street was broken only by light from the windows of the Empress and Palace saloons, and the single wall-bracket lamp in the hotel lobby. Nothing seemed out of the way. The town had quieted down. Two horses stood in front of the Palace, three before the Empress.

There would be no safety for Cotton in Antioch or on Broken Ring range as long as Red Donahue and Keno Harriman were here and alive. If they were dead, Butch Ramsay and the rest would drift away, but now Donahue and Harriman were here and very much alive. More than that, they were here to stay, because the stakes they were playing for were big. So Cotton gave the street the same careful survey that he had given streets in the past when death lurked in shadowy alley mouths, and to that care and a fast and accurate gun he owed his life. He had been through affairs like this before, but never with the odds quite so great against him, never with so little help on his side.

For more than a minute Cotton studied the street; then, satisfied that there was no enemy waiting for him, he left the hotel, moved rapidly to the corner, and turned up Lincoln Street toward the stable. The yellow light of a lantern showed through the archway. For one short interval Cotton's lank body was thrown into dark relief as he stepped inside. In that instant a gun roared from across the street. Cotton felt the hot slash of the slug along his ribs as he dropped flat, pulling his gun from leather as he fell.

Chapter Five

Wolves Attack
at Dawn

TWO MORE TIMES THE DRYGULCHER'S GUN SPOKE, RED RIB-
bons stabbing the night blackness. Slugs screamed above Cotton. This was the second time, Cotton thought as he lay there,
that Red Donahue had ordered the death of a man, and his
killers had failed. They had drawn blood, but still had failed
in their purpose.

Lamps bloomed to life as men tumbled from beds and pulled
on their pants. In a moment they'd be streaming into Lincoln
Street with lanterns, and Donahue's man would be gone from
the alley. The only reason Cotton was alive now was that he
had kept Keno Harriman and Red Donahue back on their heels
all day. That was Cotton's way of fighting, and he followed it
again. He snapped two quick shots from where he lay. Then
he came up from his prone position in a quick, upward and
sideways movement that carried him away from the door.

The man across the street fired, but he had aimed at Cotton's
gun flashes, just as Cotton had guessed he would. In doing that,
he gave his position away. Three times Cotton drove slugs at

the spot where the man was standing, placing them waist-high, and two feet apart. Quickly Cotton moved along the stable wall. He paused, shoved new loads into the cylinder, and waited, but not long. The townsmen came from Main Street: Dib Alcott the marshal, and others, but neither Donahue nor Harriman was with them.

Cotton did not move until Alcott had reached the alleyhead where the killer had stood. He watched the marshal tilt his lantern and throw the light against the back of a man who was lying face down in the street. Alcott turned him over. "It's Toad Maxon," he said, "and mighty damned dead."

Cotton came up then, casting a quick look over the dozen men standing around the body, and was surprised to see Santiam Jones and Bill Curry among them.

"He opened up on me as I went into the stable, Marshal," Cotton said. "It was luck he's lying there instead of me."

"Cotton," Santiam bellowed. "Holy smoke, where you been? I might have known if there was a gun ruckus, you'd be in it up to your neck."

"Yeah," Curry said. "I hear we missed out on Malloy's shooting. We was having a talk with . . . Yow! Dang your hide, Santiam. You know your doggone elbow's sharper'n a hound's tooth."

"Then shut up," Santiam growled.

Dib Alcott had been watching. Now he said, "Some of you boys carry the carcass over to Doc Vance. Cotton, looks like you got hit, or is that ketchup coming out of you?"

"Vinegar it'd be," Santiam said soberly, "if it's coming out of him. Vinegar with a mite of coloring in it."

"I'll mosey along to Doc's office," Cotton said. "You boys bring Redman down there, will you? I've got a pile of riding to do before morning."

"I'll consider it," Santiam said doubtfully.

"If he don't show up," Curry grunted, "you'll know he stole the critter. He's feeling too big across his seat for his britches right now. Wait'll I tell you what that blonde . . . Yow! Dang

BUCKAROO'S CODE   43

your ornery hide. If you stick that elbow into me again, I'll swing on you. So help me."

"Your tongue," Santiam growled, "is hinged in the middle, and she sure swings nice and easy on both ends. Shut up, and let's go get that animal."

Dib Alcott walked along with Cotton toward the medico's office. He asked, "What's been going on today? Is Broken Ring having a civil war?"

"Something like that," Cotton admitted.

"I hear that when I was out looking in the alley for sign of that jigger who cut down on Malloy, you and Red mighty near had it out. They say you made a remark like mebbe Keno Harriman was the one who shot Malloy, then you bluffed Donahue out of going for his gun, and left the saloon."

"That's about it," Cotton admitted. "I didn't say Harriman shot Malloy. I don't make a habit of accusing a man of murder until I know he pulled the trigger."

"Now this Toad Maxon takes a few shots at you," Alcott said thoughtfully, "and he's one of Harriman's crowd. You all work for Broken Ring. It don't make sense."

"It will one of these days," Cotton said, "when it's all washed out." He nodded at Alcott, and went into the medico's office just as the men left who had carried Toad Maxon's body into Vance's back room. "Got a little scratch on one of my ribs, Doc. Thought mebbe you could patch it up some."

Vance was a small man with a dark beard and equally dark eyes. He nodded in answer to Cotton, and said, "Pull off your shirt, son. We'll have a look."

Vance had come into the country when there were only a few scattered settlers on French Creek, and none on what was now Broken Ring range. As he cleaned the wound, he said, "Sometimes I wonder about these hombres who think they're so tough. They hire out as gunhands, and pull down fighting wages, but I've noticed that when the shooting's over, it's the working buckaroos who usually come out on top. Now take you and Toad Maxon. Maxon never was anything but a hard

44 WAYNE D. OVERHOLSER

case who drank too much, gambled away his big money, and now he's ready for boot hill. On the other hand I haven't seen you in town all summer. Why? Because you've been out doing a man's work, and now all you've got is a little meat knocked off a rib. That'll be a mite sore, son."

"I'll be lucky if it's all the meat I lose." Cotton slid into his shirt, and started buttoning it.

Doc Vance's black eyes were studying Cotton's face. Suddenly he said, "I had a little place south of here, but Malloy's got it now. I figure life's too short to scrap with a man who can afford to hire the gun crew Jackson Malloy's got. I'm guessing that wolf pack's turning on Malloy. I sure don't know of anybody else in this country who'd shoot at a man from a dark alley but some of Harriman's toughs. Just like," he jerked a thumb toward the back room, "Maxon back there. Now I've always liked the cut of your jib, Cotton. I don't know why Harriman or Donahue or whoever it is that runs the wolf pack would want you beefed, but there isn't any doubt about the fact that they do. Take my advice and light out of town. Keep moving until you're a thousand miles from here."

Cotton's grin was a sudden curved line across his dark face. "Thanks, Doc. Reckon I'll have to turn your advice down. That bunch has a good reason to want me dead. If I sloped out of here now, I'd never be able to take a good, square look at myself. Likely I'll be in to get some more holes patched up one of these days. So long, Doc."

Santiam Jones and Bill Curry were waiting outside with Cotton's roan and their own horses. "You boys riding with me?" Cotton asked as he stepped up.

"For a spell," Santiam answered.

Later, when the last lights of Antioch were hidden behind the brown slopes of the Dead Horse Hills, Bill Curry said, "I've got two sore spots where Santiam dug his elbows into me trying to make me keep my mouth shut, but, hod dang it, I'm gonna tell what I want to tell. Reckon even Santiam's skinny elbow can't get over here."

BUCKAROO'S CODE   45

"Go ahead," Santiam said disgustedly. "Spill everything you know."

"Before you boys start telling secrets," Cotton said, "mebbe you'd like to hear that I'm the new Broken Ring ramrod. Red Donahue and all of Harriman's bunch get fired tomorrow."

Santiam began to curse deeply and fervently. "Wouldn't you know it? Now wouldn't you just know that's the kind of luck I'd draw to."

"What's biting you now?" Cotton demanded. "I thought you'd kind o' like the idea."

"I like the idea fine," Santiam answered. "Go ahead, Bill. Tell him."

"We're working for that blond gal," Bill said triumphantly. "Santiam's the ramrod, and I'm the segundo. Fact is, we're the whole dang crew. She's paying us seventy-five a month."

"You mean Sandra Taney hired you two jayhoos?" Cotton demanded. "You mean she's marrying one of you?"

"Marrying one of us?" Santiam howled with laughter. "Son, she sure wouldn't waste herself on a homely galoot like me. As for that keg of taller riding on the other side of you, why, I can't believe yet she'd even hire him, let alone pay him as much as she's paying me. No sir, she ain't marrying one of us. She's just aiming to work the tail off us."

"Now let's get this straight," Cotton said as if he still didn't believe what he was hearing. "This Taney gal hires you for what? She hasn't got no spread."

"I'll tell you how it was," Santiam said, "and I'm plumb sorry I didn't know Malloy was gonna get smart and make you ramrod, or we wouldn't have gone to work for a gal. I was glad to get off Broken Ring, and the dinero she was talking about looked awful good. It would keep Bill in eating and drinking for a couple days or more."

"All right, all right," Cotton said impatiently. "What's the deal?"

"Well, we was talking to Miss Sandra when you was having the trouble with Donahue in the Empress. Say, I'd like to have seen that. I dunno why our luck's running so bad. I'd give a purty to see you back Red up like you did."

"Listen," Cotton shouted, "if you don't tell . . ."

"Yeah, sure, I'm getting at it. I reckon she kind o' liked your looks, son. She saw us eating together. That's how she spotted us. Anyhow, we was walking along in front of the hotel, and she said she wanted to talk to us. She took us up to her room, and told us she wanted a spread. She wanted it purty close to Broken Ring, and she wants to make Mr. Jackson Malloy a lot of trouble. Fact is, she'd like to bust him flat."

"That's plumb interesting," Cotton said, remembering Malloy had refused to talk about the blond girl.

"Sure is," Santiam said proudly, "and we're the ones that's gonna be fighting Malloy. She trusts us. She wants a place that has a cabin, and some water. Well, water being what it is, I couldn't think of no place but Slow Spring. It ain't much water, but . . ."

"Slow Spring," Cotton roared. "Santiam, are you crazy? Except for Cold Creek it's the only water within ten miles of the Wishbone Mountains. Malloy couldn't let that go. Besides, you filed on it."

"Yep," Santiam said placidly. "I ain't forgot. I figgered I'd sell to Miss Sandra."

"Malloy won't stand for that," Cotton said angrily. "You can't do it, Santiam."

"The hell I can't," Santiam returned. "Tell you what. You quit Broken Ring, and go to work for Miss Sandra. Me and Bill are getting our soogans, and riding on down to Slow Spring. We'll clean the cabin out so she can live in it. Then we're heading down to Nevada to bring back some beef she bought."

"That's a good idea," Bill Curry said thoughtfully. "You can be ramrod, Cotton. Santiam wouldn't be no good anyhow. I'd sure rather be segundo to a good man than a bean pole like Santiam. You know, Cotton, Miss Sandra was playing with a penholder when we was talking to her, and once when she held it up in front of her, she plumb lost Santiam behind it. She thought he'd walked out. Yessir, that's a fact. He's so doggone skinny he actually hid behind that there penholder."

Cotton did not smile. They rode in silence, Cotton trying to see where Sandra Taney fitted into the picture, and the others thinking that Cotton was angry because they had quit Broken Ring. When they reached the fork in the road that swung east to Broken Ring, Cotton reined up. He said, "Well, boys, good riding. It's a long trip to Nevada." Disappointment was sharp in his voice. These were the two men he had counted on. With them gone, anything might happen when Malloy told Donahue he was fired.

"I reckon we'll be seeing you," Santiam said gruffly. "I sure didn't think it would work this way. We thought mebbe we could talk you into working for Miss Sandra. Fact is . . ."

"Shut up," Bill cut in. "Now who's got the tongue that's swinging free on both ends?"

"I'm gonna tell him," Santiam said doggedly, "no matter what she said. Miss Sandra offered us one hundred dollars apiece if we got you to come and work for her. Of course she said you was to be ramrod, and I'm thinking she's gonna have a purty nice place. We're gonna build her a lean-to. Sort of a bedroom for her, I reckon. Now if things don't go on Broken Ring like they oughta, you let us know. Might be you'll need a couple of good guns. Of course Bill there ain't no account, but he might stand in front of you and stop the bullets."

"Huh," Bill snapped, "you sure wouldn't be no good for that. Them slugs would go crazy trying to connect up with you."

"So long, boys," Cotton said, and swung Redman toward Fred Flagg's FF.

A cold night wind came down from the Cascades. Around Cotton the coyotes lifted their mournful howls. Above him was the clear, star-burned sky. There had been a rain here but a few hours before, and in the air was the full, stirring incense of the sage. In that hour Cotton's thoughts ran freely, and in him were questions for which he had no answers. He thought of June Flagg, and the choice she had made. He thought of Sandra Taney, and her strange request, and her still stranger ambition to start a ranch here under Jackson Malloy's nose, of her wanting to break him, and he wondered what lay behind.

Then Cotton thought of his own youth, and his father, as he and his mother had found him, stretched upon the gravel of a river bank, a bullet between his shoulders. He thought of his mother, and how she had died, trying to make a living for them. The picture of Luke Bray's burned cabin and the two graves came to him, and the hatred that he felt for Red Donahue was a deep and poisonous thing.

Some of the hatred passed from him then, for no man could live and breathe and ride in a wild, beautiful country like this, and see and feel that beauty without having some of it become a part of him. Yet men like Red Donahue did live and breathe and ride through these pines, see these mountains, and look upon these rivers, and never know there was peace and beauty here. This puzzled Cotton. He thought about it, and wondered why he had not become like Donahue. Why did he live by a different code than did Red Donahue and Keno Harriman?

This question Cotton Drennan could not answer. He only knew that his life was being offered in defense of the principles he considered right and just. June Flagg might marry Abernethy for his money, yet she might need Cotton Drennan's help, the kind of help a pilgrim like Abernethy could never give her. Cotton would give her that help. Why, he did not know, but he would give it. At a time like this his mind grappled with questions that no mortal can ever answer. What was beyond this life, and what lies ahead in eternity more than in this wind-swept, massive earth? The answers seemed to be here before him, out there somewhere beyond his reach. Then he was thinking again of June Flagg. Perhaps the answers he sought were found in the love of a man for a woman, the kind of love that would never be in the heart of a man like Red Donahue.

BUCKAROO'S CODE 49

Then Cotton was through the pines, and tipping down the steep slope to the meadow that held the FF buildings: the log cabin, the corrals, the small, tight barn. He was twenty yards from the corral when Fred Flagg's voice cut through the mountain silence, "Hold up till I get a look at you."

"It's Cotton." He reined up, and waited.

Fred Flagg let out a gust of air. "I'm glad it's you, Cotton. I thought sure as hell it was Red Donahue. Light and rest your saddle, son. June and me just got in."

Cotton stripped gear from his roan, and put him into the corral. June was standing behind Cotton, and when he turned he saw the light oval of her face. She had been looking at him, judging him, perhaps, alongside Jackson Malloy and J. Francis Abernethy. For just a moment they stood that way, facing each other, two dark shapes in the starlight. Cotton wondered if the girl had been asking herself the same questions he had been pondering as she had sat beside her father in the buckboard. There had been the same sky and the same stars above them, the same wind upon their faces.

Then Cotton turned away. No, June Flagg would not be thinking those same thoughts. She had chosen freely, and love had not been her choice. She had said, or practically so, that she had gone with Jackson Malloy tonight because he had money. Then it had been Abernethy, who had more money than Malloy. Yet it did not add up. Malloy had said he had asked her to marry him, and she would have none of him.

"June," Cotton said softly, coming back to where the girl stood, "I've got to know. Is it Malloy that you want to marry, or Abernethy? Are you trying to buy . . ."

"No." It was that simple. One word. One syllable.

Cotton's arms opened to her then, and she was in them, and he was kissing her, and the stars were wheeling around in a crazy fashion above them. There was that moment in which he tasted the sweetness of her lips, that moment when her soft body was in his arms held tightly against him, one sacred, beautiful moment when the answers to all these questions he had asked himself were here almost within reach.

Then the moment was shattered when Fred Flagg called from the cabin door, "You kids gonna stand out there in the cold all night?"

June pulled away from him. "We'd better go in," she whispered.

They walked together toward the cabin, slowly, their arms around each other, the afterglow of their kiss a great warmth surrounding them. Flagg had lighted a lamp. He stood now in the doorway, a square-bodied man throwing a shadow across the yard, a sober look on his face as he watched them.

"Mebbe you two have made up," he said hopefully, as if it were a little more than he could expect. "I told June I didn't want no money-grubbers like Jackson Malloy marrying into the Flagg family just so they could get a watering place on the river. Likewise I didn't want no society dude like J. Francis Abernethy showing his ugly mug around here."

"Dad," June cried. "Don't talk that way in front of Cotton."

"Why not?" her father demanded. "Any man who comes around here courting the purtiest girl on White River has gotta be a scrapping buckaroo. Looks to me like this boy can qualify. What's more, we've got a chance to build a mighty good spread out of the FF. I can use a good hand, and when a man marries you, he gets a half interest . . ."

Fred Flagg gasped, his body flinching under the impact of a heavy slug. He grabbed at his shirt front, then sprawled back into the cabin. From somewhere down along the river came the sharp crack of a Winchester.

Chapter Six
Siege

COTTON ACTED INSTINCTIVELY. HE GAVE JUNE A VIOLENT push that shoved her through the door and sent her sprawling full length on the cabin floor. He leaped after her, grabbed Fred Flagg's still form, and pulled him behind the shelter of the solid log wall. Outside, other rifles had begun firing from along the river and from the pines north of the barn. Cotton heard the shriek of slugs through the doorway, heard the slap of them into the logs.

"Dad!" June cried. "Is he hurt bad?"

"Bad enough, I reckon," Cotton answered, "judging from the way he went down. Don't start moving around till I get that door shut, and hug the floor. We're gonna get a lot of lead through them windows."

The door opened to the other side. The lamp was on a table in the center of the room directly in front of the door. To shut the door, Cotton would have to show himself in the light, so he took what seemed the least chance of getting hit. He stepped quickly to the opposite side of the doorway; for that brief instant of movement his lank body was silhouetted against the lamp. His appearance brought a belated stream of bullets through the doorway, but the raiders had been too slow. Cotton swung the heavy door shut, and dropped the bar.

June had been kneeling beside her father. Now she looked up as Cotton turned to her. She whispered, "He's dying."

Cotton bent over Flagg. "I don't think so," he said, shaking his head. The bullet had smashed through Flagg's ribs and angled out through his side. "Get some bandages on him, June. Mebbe you can stop the bleeding some. I think he'll make it if we get him to Doc Vance soon enough. Trouble is there's a big bunch of coyotes outside, judging from the amount of shooting. Hard to tell when we can get out of here."

Outside they were keeping up the same steady firing. Once a bullet found a hole in the chinking, and screamed the width of the cabin. As Cotton took Flagg's Winchester down from the wall, he said, "I'll burn a little powder just to show 'em we ain't dead."

"Dad bored a hole beside each of the windows," June told him. "He thought this was coming, so he got ready for it the best he could. What he was afraid of most was that they'd bushwhack him and I'd be alone in the cabin."

It was strange, Cotton thought, that Flagg had given no indication when they had talked in town that he saw this coming. Apparently Cotton had succeeded in doing nothing beyond making Flagg think he was working hand in glove with Malloy. Cotton levered a shell into the Winchester, and slipped the barrel through the hole. Ribbons of flame were coming spasmodically from the river. He raked their position with rifle fire, laying his bullets two feet apart. There was no real shelter along the river bank, and Cotton thought his chance of driving a slug home was good. When the Winchester was empty, he asked, "Any more shells?"

"Over there in the corner," June answered.

Cotton filled the magazine, and stepped back to his former position. This time he held his fire until he caught the shadow

BUCKAROO'S CODE

of a man moving from the river toward the barn. He shot fast three times, saw the man drop flat on his belly, but he could not be sure whether he had hit the raider or not. After that the firing ceased except for an occasional shot from the river.

"They're not shooting much," Cotton said somberly, "but it's a cinch Harriman isn't pulling his wolves off. I don't like the looks of this." Turning from the window he saw that June had finished the bandaging, and had thrown a quilt over Flagg. "It's mighty close to dawn. They'll want to finish us off before then."

"There's one way they can get us out of here," June said. "They can burn the cabin."

Cotton swore softly. They would be caught like rats. If they tried to make a run for it, they would be cut down long before they could reach cover. Besides, there was Fred Flagg to think of.

"Well," Cotton said, grinning crookedly at June, "it's been a nice life. Only trouble is I had a couple of chores to do before I cashed in."

"Is Malloy out there?" June asked.

"No. Malloy's in bed in the hotel. Somebody tried to drygulch him in town, but they got him a little high. I reckon it's Harriman's crowd."

"But it's Malloy who wants us out of here," June said.

Cotton smiled grimly. "He's got plenty of trouble without taking on any more. Seems like Donahue's got an idea he wants Broken Ring. I've got a hunch he's the one giving the orders. If Malloy gets beefed, which is likely to happen, Donahue takes over. Mebbe he figgers on making the sale to Abernethy. With this place open, Broken Ring could be made into a big spread. Otherwise it's like most ranches in this country: lots of grass and not much water. Anyhow, it doesn't look like we can do much about saving the FF or our hides, either."

"It isn't that bad," June said quickly. "About a year ago Malloy began trying to buy Dad out. With Harriman's gun crew chasing the other homesteaders out of the country, Dad figured he would be next, so he moved the cabin over a cave. You know how this country is. There's caves everywhere."

"You mean . . ."

"That's right." June threw a rag rug into a corner and lifted a trap door. "Move that slab of rock, Cotton. It's right here."

Cotton laid down the Winchester, and stepped to where the girl stood. Time had nearly run out for them. The crackling of flames overhead told him the raiders had succeeded in firing the roof.

"I should have killed Donahue when I had a chance," Cotton muttered as he lifted the slab of rock. He stared into a black hole. "What's down there?"

"It's not deep right here," June answered, "but it widens out and runs toward the river. We've got ammunition and food down there, and other things we really wanted to save, like my mother's picture." June slid off into the cave, and stood with the top of her head level with the cabin floor. She held up her hands. "Give me the lamp. Then let Dad down."

Cotton gave her the lamp, handed her the Winchester, and gently lowered Flagg into the cave mouth. Above him the fire had eaten a hole into the roof, and sparks were beginning to fall into the cabin. Cotton moved the rock slab partly over the hole, and dropped through. Then, with his feet on the floor of the cave, he raised his hands, and shoved the slab into place.

"Carry Dad over here, Cotton," June said. "We fixed some pine boughs for a bed, but we never thought he would be like this." She stood aside while Cotton moved Flagg, then she covered him with blankets, and stood up, her face showing the worry that was in her. "You think he'll be all right?"

"Depends on how soon we get out of here. Chances are they'll wait till the cabin is down, and they'll vamose. They'll figger we'll be purty well baked, and they won't worry about us."

"But the barn and the horses? We can't get him to town if they take the buckboard."

BUCKAROO'S CODE   55

"They won't be hanging around here very long," Cotton said grimly. "Somebody might see them. There's always a chance they'll go too far, and folks around Antioch will get enough sand in their craw to send for the sheriff. Donahue won't want that. Besides, Abernethy or whoever is gonna run Broken Ring will need what's here. No use busting up things anybody can use. Chances are they wouldn't have burned the cabin if there was any other way of boosting us out."

June stood looking down at her father, and Cotton, sensing her feelings, stepped away. He explored the cave, saw that it ran directly west and that the floor dipped gradually toward the river. Fifty yards from where Flagg lay the cave stopped, but Cotton, looking at it, decided that it was filled with sand beyond that point, and probably went a long way if a man wanted to dig it out. He had seen many caves similar to this in central Oregon, resulting, he had been told, from volcanic action of an earlier age. He went back to where Flagg lay, thinking it a grim joke that nature had provided the only means of escape from the human vultures outside.

"He's breathing easier now," June said. She looked at Cotton, and spread her hands wearily. "It's strange how much trouble there is in life, all because of greed. There was no reason why we should have been bothered. Dad never harmed anyone."

Above them they could hear the brisk crackling of the flames. Cotton jerked his thumb toward the rock slab that covered the mouth of the cave. "Like that," he said bitterly. He stood looking at June, thinking she had not told him she loved him. Neither had he told her he loved her. Nor was this moment, with Fred Flagg lying there, perhaps dying, the time. So Cotton only said, "Funny about Fred. When I was talking to him in town he didn't say he figgered anything was gonna happen. Seemed to think I was trying to bluff him into taking Malloy's offer."

"He did think that," June admitted. "We talked about it when we were coming home. Dad heard about your trouble with Donahue and Harriman, and he changed his mind. Dad's awful stubborn, Cotton. When he came here three years ago there were several homesteaders scattered around between the river and the desert, and as far north as Antioch. Then Malloy showed up with Harriman's gun-packing crew, and Dad watched the homesteaders get chased out one after the other. Then there was nobody left but us and the Brays, and they were clear out in the edge of the desert at Sand Spring."

"If it hadn't been for you, Malloy would have got rid of your dad a long time ago," Cotton said. "I had a talk with him tonight before I left town. The last thing he said was that whatever happens, he did not want you hurt. I dunno." Cotton shook his head. "Mebbe I've pegged Malloy all wrong. Mebbe it's been Donahue who's done the skunk tricks I've laid to Malloy."

"You don't need to play John Alden for Jackson Malloy," June cried angrily. "I would never marry him. He's been told enough times. If we ever get out of here you can tell him that."

"He knows it," Cotton said.

"Then why . . ."

"Because Malloy told me to tell you," Cotton said wearily. "Because Malloy sent me out here to tell Fred he had to sell to save his neck, and that Malloy would give him any price within reason. I reckon Malloy had a hunch what Harriman meant to do, or what Donahue was gonna tell him to do."

"I see," June said, icily.

"Malloy isn't a killer, June," Cotton went on, not sensing the change in her. "Donahue is, and it looks to me like he's been running the homesteaders off to carry out his own ideas. Since Abernethy showed up, Donahue has got to push this through. I figger he's been putting the blame on Malloy. Now that there isn't any more time, he aims to beef Malloy, push you folks off, and wind up the deal with Abernethy. It's an old game dressed up in new clothes, with plenty in it for

BUCKAROO'S CODE

Donahue, Harriman, and the whole wolf pack. Beats holding up banks."

"I thought you didn't like Malloy," June cried.

"I don't," Cotton said quickly. "I don't like a man who builds a ranch for no better reason than to sell it to some Eastern dude, but right now I'm into a fight with Donahue and Harriman, and I'm plumb up to my neck. Either I get help, or I'm a gone goose. The way the cards are falling, Malloy is the only help I can get." He looked sharply at June then, realizing a change had come over her. "Why the third degree, June? You seemed to be having a good time with Malloy yesterday."

"If you had the sense of a wall-eyed maverick," June snapped, "you would know why I was with Malloy. He has told me a dozen times he loved me. Asked me to marry him, but when this Abernethy fellow shows up, Malloy used me as bait to help him sell Broken Ring. He didn't fool me a bit, but I had hoped he'd let us alone if I did what he wanted."

"But you didn't mean it about Malloy's money. You . . . you aren't that way, June. You told me when you kissed me . . ."

"Any girl can make a mistake in kissing a man," June said coldly. "No, I didn't mean it about Malloy's money. When I marry, it will be because I love a man, and for no other reason. I didn't think you'd come out here to tell me how much Malloy thinks of me. I say it is Malloy who told Harriman's men to attack us. I don't believe there's any trouble between him and Donahue. I think the whole thing is a lying, trumped-up, dirty scheme to make us sell out, Cotton Drennan, and I didn't think you'd stoop to anything as rotten as that. I'm sorry I kissed you."

June whirled away, went back to where her father lay, and sat beside him. Cotton did not follow her. For a time he stood motionless, staring at her, unable to think. Then he sat down, his back against the cold wall of the cave, and built a smoke. He pulled a match across the rock, and held the flame to his cigarette. He remembered telling Santiam Jones and Bill Curry that a man who tries to figure out women is building himself up for a headache. Gazing at June's back, he thought sourly that he had not known the half of it then.

An hour passed. Two hours. Neither Cotton nor June spoke. There was no sound but Fred Flagg's hard breathing, and the occasional scratch of a match head across the rock wall as Cotton lighted a cigarette. Overhead the crackle of flames had died. Presently June rose, and faced him. "Do you think they're still there?" she asked, her voice utterly lacking in its usual friendly warmth.

"Mebbe," Cotton answered. He put his hands to the slab of rock above him, and drew them away quickly. He said, "Still hot."

June picked up a pair of gloves from a pile of boxes stacked along the wall. "Try these. They're Dad's."

Cotton slipped on the gloves. With a quick motion he shoved the rock slab to one side, and stepped away as a small avalanche of coals and ashes fell through to the cave floor. For a time Cotton stood motionless, listening, gun palmed. It was full daylight now. Hearing nothing, Cotton moved back under the opening. By standing tiptoe, he could see across the floor of the cabin. Some of the walls were standing, charred memorials to Red Donahue's cruel and vicious nature.

It was raining again. When Cotton put his hand out, and felt the wet ashes, he realized there had been a heavy shower, and that the fire had been put out before the cabin had been completely burned.

Cotton stepped away, replacing his gun, and said, "I don't see nobody. It's been raining, and I think the ashes are cooled down enough so we can get out. Chances are they waited till they figgered there wouldn't be anything left alive inside. Then they lit a shuck for Broken Ring. Keno Harriman will be plumb surprised when he sees us. So will Red Donahue." He pinned his gaze on June's face. "And with you thinking me the world's biggest liar, you'll think Malloy will be surprised to see us."

"I didn't say you were the world's biggest liar," June said quickly.

BUCKAROO'S CODE   59

"You might as well. I never could follow the kind of thinking a woman does. Looks to me like you'd see I was telling it straight when I stayed inside. I didn't dare take a chance on poking my head out. What's more, I thought you knew me well enough, and mebbe thought enough of me to know I wouldn't lie to you, but I was sure wrong."

June said nothing while Cotton pulled a box under the opening, and stepped up on it. He said, "Hand the Winchester up to me. I'll get the buckboard if they've left the team here," and crawled up to the cabin floor. He plowed through the ashes in three long steps, and paused outside what had been the door. Smoke still hung low over the meadow, and with the smell of it was the tang of the wet sage. The barn had been untouched. Beside it was the buckboard, in the exact spot where Flagg had left it the night before. Cotton's roan, June's bay mare, and Flagg's team were still in the corral.

For a long moment Cotton stood without moving, eyes scanning with habitual thoroughness the river and the pines north of the barn from which the rifle fire had come the night before. He circled the remains of the cabin, went on to the barn, and searched it. Finding no one, he left it and stood outside, making his scrutiny with great care. Then, convinced that the raiders had left no one behind, he saddled Redman and June's mare, harnessed the team, and hitched them to the buckboard. He tied June's mare behind the buckboard, and drove to the cabin.

"Nobody seems to be around," Cotton said, lowering himself through the cave opening. "I've got the buckboard hitched up. Reckon we can move."

"How can we get him out of here?" June asked, motioning to her father.

"We'll put a rope under his arms, and pull him up. It's just as well he's still out." Cotton moved Flagg, laying him down under the cave opening, and tying the rope around him that June handed him. "Anything else down here you want to take to town?"

"No," June answered. "Just the quilts to cover him with."

"I'll take them now," Cotton said. He climbed out, carried the quilts to the buckboard, and fixed a bed. Then he returned, took the end of the rope June handed him, and, after kicking away the ashes around the edge, pulled Flagg up through the hole. He turned, drew Flagg's limp body over his shoulder, and carried him to the buckboard.

June was beside Cotton almost as soon as he reached the buckboard. He said, "I was going back after you."

"I can manage," the girl said shortly.

"Sure there's nothing else you want?"

June shook her head.

"If you don't tell anybody how you lived through that fire, nobody'll know about the cave, and your things won't be touched."

"It won't be me that'll tell anybody," June said pointedly.

Cotton swung on his heel, the anger in him close to boiling over. He laid the slab back, toed ashes over it, and returned to the buckboard. June was in the seat, the lines in her hands, the Winchester beside her.

"I'll ride along behind," Cotton said curtly, not looking at June, and went after Redman.

Chapter Seven

"I'm Gonna Kill You, Cotton"

IT WAS DUSK BY THE TIME JUNE DROVE INTO ANTIOCH. DURing the long trip into town Cotton had not spoken to her. He had been given time to think, and the thoughts in him were poisonous and bitter. There seemed to be no understanding to it. June had kissed him as only a woman in love would kiss a man. Then, within an hour of that time, she had not believed him; had accused him of playing Malloy's dirty scheme to get Fred Flagg to sell. Now, hours later as they came into town, some of the pain that June's words had brought had died in him.

Other memories had come to Cotton; the murder of Luke Bray and his wife, the bitter hatred Red Donahue and Keno Harriman felt for him, Sandra Taney's proposal of marriage and the mystery of what lay between her and Jackson Malloy. He had thought of Santiam Jones and Bill Curry working for the blond girl, and had asked himself if he had made a mistake when he had not taken her offer. He owed nothing to Jackson Malloy. Now he owed nothing to June Flagg; yet he knew he would do nothing differently if he had these last twenty-four hours to live over. He knew, too, that he loved June Flagg and would go on loving her, and he cursed himself for a fool. His mind had gone back over all this time after time, and always came again to June Flagg. Somehow he had to make her believe him.

June pulled up in front of the medico's office. Cotton carried Flagg inside, and laid him on a bed in a back room. He put the horses away, and when he came back Vance and June were in the office.

"If he doesn't get infection, he'll be all right," the medico was saying. "It isn't a bad bullet hole. Maybe you didn't know it," he nodded at June, "but Fred hasn't been feeling well. He figured he had a fight coming, but he was too danged stubborn to sell out and git. He claimed this was the place he'd been looking for all his life. The upshot of it is he's been worrying himself sick."

"Let's go eat, June," Cotton said, taking the girl's arm.

"I'm not hungry," June said, pulling away from Cotton.

"How'd you two and Fred get into this scrap?" the medico demanded.

"I went out there to see 'em," Cotton answered. "Malloy didn't order the raid, but he had a hunch what was gonna happen, so he sent me out to warn 'em. I hadn't much more'n got there when they hit us. There isn't anything we can do for Fred now, is there, Doc? We haven't had a thing to eat since last night. Fact is, I can't remember what grub looks like."

Doc Vance grinned. "Go on, June. I'll be here looking after Fred. I don't want two more patients on my hands."

Again Cotton gripped June's arm, and this time she went with him. Sandra Taney was in the hotel lobby as they walked through it into the dining room. Cotton lifted his Stetson, and spoke to her, noting the curious look she gave June. Sandra opened her mouth as if she were going to say something to Cotton, but he appeared not to see, and went on with June.

Later, when they were through eating, Cotton said, "I'm going back to Broken Ring tomorrow. Thought I'd stay in town tonight."

June nodded, and rose. Outside Cotton said, "I know this has been purty tough on you. After you get time to think, mebbe you'll see things a little different. I didn't lie to you, June. I didn't come out there to play John Alden for Malloy. He knows you'll never love him, but I think he's telling it straight when he says he thinks enough of you that he wouldn't order a raid. You can believe that or not, but one thing you've got to believe, June. I did not come out there to run a sandy on Fred so he'd sell to Malloy."

June raised her eyes to Cotton then. She said simply, "I don't know what to believe, Cotton. I have never trusted Jackson Malloy. I didn't think you'd have any part knowingly in carrying out his dirty schemes. I'm . . . I'm sorry I said what I did back there this morning. It's just that I . . . I thought you . . ." She looked away then, and swallowed. "Thank you for what you did, Cotton." She turned into the medico's office, and went on through it into the room where her father lay, leaving the gulf between them as wide as it had been. Cotton, staring after her, considered how far a man could bend his pride, and knew he could go no farther. June had not said she believed him.

"Cotton," Doc Vance called, and came out of his office. "I'm going to see Dib Alcott. He's only the town marshal, but by hokey, it's got to the place where we've got to have some law down here."

"Dib won't do nothing," Cotton said, and started to turn away.

"Hold on." Vance caught Cotton's arm, and turned him back. "Who did this job?"

"I dunno," Cotton answered. "It was dark, and I didn't get a chance to see."

"Who do you think?"

"I don't reckon there's much doubt. I figger it was Harriman's bunch. I had a talk with Malloy last night, but I don't think he had any part in it. Mebbe Red Donahue gave the order."

"How'd you save your hides?"

Cotton grinned mirthlessly. "Let June tell you that. Doc, did Malloy go back to Broken Ring?"

"This morning with Abernethy," Vance answered. "Where are you going now?"

"Back to Broken Ring."

"Don't be a damned fool," the doctor said bluntly. "Sometimes a man can't help being part of a fool, but you don't have to be a complete one. You go out there, and Donahue or Harriman or Butch Ramsay or some of the rest will put a window in your skull right now."

"I've got to go, Doc," Cotton said. "There's a lot going on around here folks don't know. Mebbe I can't handle it, but I've got to try. I'll admit I'm a damn fool. Won't even argue about it."

"Donahue and Harriman were in town looking for you this morning," Vance said. "Along before noon."

"Just to make it look good," Cotton said thoughtfully. "They burned Flagg's cabin, and they figgered I burned with it. They'll be plumb surprised when I show up. See you later, Doc. I'm staying in town tonight."

Cotton signed for a room in the hotel, and as he turned from the desk, he almost stepped on Sandra Taney's toes. She did not move back as she said, "I want to talk to you, Cotton. You knew I did a while ago, but you went on."

"I'm working for Broken Ring," Cotton said a little roughly, "and I ain't interested in a job or getting married." He paused, and added, "For money."

The girl's eyes dropped momentarily. "I . . . I'm sorry about that. We will forget it. I want only to hire you to run the ranch I'm going to have at Slow Spring. Santiam Jones and Bill Curry have already gone there, and I've sent a wagonload out."

"I know," Cotton said, "about Santiam and Bill."

"I have heard it told what happened here last night," Sandra said. "For the year that you have been in this country you were one of eight or ten punchers riding for Broken Ring. Then, for no apparent reason, you started fighting and within a matter of hours you have become a legend. I want you. I'll pay you well."

"There are other men . . ."

"No one else will do."

Sandra raised her eyes to him. They were blue eyes, light blue, and there was much knowledge in them. In this girl was the power to hold a man once she had gained him. She was wearing a blue dress that clung tightly at waist and breast; her black hat was small, and below it dropping behind her head was her yellow-gold hair. On her doll-like face, Cotton saw, was the great determination which was so much a part of this girl. For one brief moment Cotton thought of June Flagg, and how different she was from Sandra Taney, and he wondered if again he was being a fool.

Then Cotton said, "I'm sorry, ma'am. I can't take the job. I've given my word to Malloy." He stepped around her, and went up the stairs.

The fatigue of long hours in the saddle was deep in Cotton. He slept until it was full daylight, and wondered sourly why he had not wakened sooner. He had breakfast at Big Nose Charlie's, and grinned when the restaurant man said, "You sure turned out to be hell on high, red wheels, Cotton. Didn't know there was a fighting man like you on White River. What you been eating, bear meat?"

"That's right. Three times a day. Raw."

Cotton got Redman and left town by the south road. He had no idea what he'd find at Broken Ring. He should have been there yesterday, and he wondered what Jackson Malloy would say to him. Malloy might be dead by now. Or more likely he was waiting until Cotton showed up, and had done nothing.

Cotton was halfway between the Dead Horse Hills and Broken Ring when he saw two horsemen ahead of him on a ridge. He could not tell who they were, and he thought some of taking a wide circle to avoid them. If it were Harriman or

66   WAYNE D. OVERHOLSER

Donahue they would set a bushwhack trap, but if it were Al
Rhyman and Bud Kroft or any of the rest of the Broken Ring
buckaroos, he would find out what had happened. He thought
about it for a time, and decided to stay on the road. Easing
his Colt in leather, he kept on.

When Cotton reached the top of the ridge he saw no one.
He reined up and, studying the tracks for a moment, saw that
they left the road and took off through the junipers. That didn't
look right, but again it might be Rhyman or some of the other
buckaroos who had seen him, and not recognized him. He
was still sitting his saddle, undecided what to do, when Red
Donahue's voice cut through the morning silence, "Don't make
a move, Cotton, or I'll drill you as sure as hell's hot."

Slowly Cotton turned his head. To his right and on the
opposite side of the road from which the horse tracks had
gone a tall upthrust of lava lifted from the sand. Behind it
was Red Donahue. Cotton couldn't see him, but he could
see the barrel of the six-gun showing through a small hole
in the lava wall. Apparently Donahue and whoever was with
him had turned off the road to the left, ridden south a short
distance, crossed the road again and had come back to hole
up in the lava. That was the sort of tricky gun trap a man
like Red Donahue would think of, and Cotton, sitting his
saddle without motion, wondered why Donahue had not shot
him.

Another man said, "Keep him covered, Red," and stepped
into view from behind the lava. It was J. Francis Abernethy,
a gun in his hand, his high-boned face the impassive one of a
man about to do a job for which he has no personal feeling.
This was not like Red Donahue, to hold Cotton under his gun
and not kill him. Neither was it like an Eastern dude to hold
a gun on him, as Abernethy was doing.

"A surprise," Cotton murmured. "I didn't expect to see you
traveling with a coyote like Red."

"Get down," Abernethy ordered. "Keep your hands away
from your gun." When Cotton had obeyed, Abernethy went on,

BUCKAROO'S CODE   67

"Now take it easy, and perhaps you won't get hurt. Unbuckle your belt, and let it drop."

Again Cotton obeyed. Donahue had not moved from behind the lava. Cotton knew too well how small a pretext the Broken Ring ramrod would need to kill him. The millionaire's presence was probably the only reason Donahue had not killed him at once.

"Good," Abernethy said. "Now step away."

Only after Cotton had obeyed this order did Red Donahue step from behind the lava. He came close, his green eyes mocking. "I've never seen a jasper who was harder to kill than you, Cotton, but I reckon you can die same as anybody else. Mebbe you're too tough to burn, but you sure as hell ain't too tough to die when you get a slug in your brisket."

"We're in no hurry," Abernethy said.

"No use beating around the bush," Donahue complained. "This jigger has got under my hide once too often. I was kind o' sorry to hear he burned up in Flagg's cabin. I've been counting on . . ."

"All right, Red," Abernethy said patiently.

The millionaire's blue eyes did not waver from Cotton's face. There was in him now a self-possession, a cool kind of calculating arrogance, that Cotton had not seen before. It struck Cotton that here, along with this cruel pattern of murder, greed, and sinister scheming that was slowly being unfolded, was J. Francis Abernethy's own carefully thought-out plan that might be as vicious as anything Red Donahue and Keno Harriman had been able to think up. Yet why should Abernethy, a millionaire, need to have a part in the things that were happening on White River if he had come here only to buy Broken Ring? It was possible that he was not the real Abernethy at all, but an imposter claiming to be Abernethy for some reason of his own. Cotton considered that thought briefly, and decided against it. Jackson Malloy was not a man who could be fooled easily.

68   WAYNE D. OVERHOLSER

"Well," Cotton said at last, "you seem to be looking me over purty well. Mebbe it would be all right now if I'd mosey on to Broken Ring."

"No," Abernethy said quickly. "I'm not one to be hurried. That's why I don't make mistakes. On the other hand, a man has to know what's happening, or waiting won't keep him from making mistakes. Now I think I've got the picture pretty well in mind except for one thing. Why have you decided to get tough? The way I get it you were just drifting around, rode in here and got a job. For a year you've been a cowpuncher, and a good one. Nothing more. You left all the fighting to Keno Harriman's crowd. Now, for no reason that anyone knows, you've been making trouble for everybody, starting in the Empress when you braced Keno Hariman. What's it all about?"

Cotton shrugged. "Seems like I've been asked that before."

"By whom?"

"Jackson Malloy," Cotton said quickly, watching Donahue's face. "He was wondering who tried to beef him."

Donahue grinned. "He shouldn't have to think too hard on that, which ain't neither here nor there. The point is you're close to seeing hell. You'll be getting a good, close view. How do you like the idea, Cotton?"

"You'll be there, too, Red," Cotton answered coolly. "Mebbe not much behind me."

"You haven't answered my question, Drennan," Abernethy said. "I want to know what changed you."

"Mebbe I haven't changed," Cotton returned. "I didn't have nothing to fight for before."

"What have you got to fight for now?"

"Why, I guess you'd say justice. Nobody gets justice in a country like this unless he fights for it. I happen to know a homesteader who lived with his wife out on the desert. They wasn't bothering anybody. Malloy hadn't given any order to have 'em pushed off, but somebody goes out there, kills both of 'em, and burns the cabin. Now I'm guessing Red there,"

BUCKAROO'S CODE 69

he nodded at Donahue, "and Harriman was the ones that did it. When the sign's right, and I don't have a couple of galoots holding their irons on me, I'll do a little squaring up for that man and his wife."

"I see," Abernethy said. "And perhaps you sort of like June Flagg?"

"That's right," Cotton admitted. "I still do."

"Hold on," Donahue said. "You mean you did like June Flagg."

"I still like her," Cotton said, grinning contemptuously at Donahue. "Your lead-slinging toughs aint' too smart, Red. June is still alive. It'll take a little more than just setting up a bushwhack trap to get FF."

"But Keno said they burned the cabin," Donahue snarled. "Said they stayed there till nothing was left but the walls. Keno claimed nobody got out. How'd you do it?"

"Look, Abernethy," Cotton said harshly. "You're supposed to be a millionaire. You're supposed to come from the East where they know a little bit about keeping wolves off other people's throats. How come you're tied up with a coyote like Donahue? He sure isn't making any bones about what's going on."

"No, he isn't," Abernethy agreed, "but that is not the point. I like you, Drennan. I know a man when I see one, and I'd rather have you on my side than half a dozen of Harriman's trigger trippers. From what I hear, you took care of yourself in Antioch the other night. You set Harriman and Red and the rest of them back on their heels. I need fighting men, Drennan. Are you interested in an offer?"

"Why would you need fighting men?" Cotton asked. "I thought you wanted a ranch where you could hunt and fish."

"That's right," Abernethy agreed, "but a spread of this size always needs fighting men. What do you say?"

"I say no," Cotton answered. "I've got a job to do for Malloy, and I couldn't do it fighting on your side. Not till you buy Broken Ring. When you do, and you fire this pack of lead throwers that Harriman runs, then I'll say yes."

Abernethy rubbed a closely shaven cheek. He said thoughtfully, "I've got my own plans, Drennan, concerning Harriman and his bunch. It would seem that most of Broken Ring's troubles are due to him."

"And Red." Cotton jerked a thumb at Donahue. "If Malloy was a real cattleman, Red would have gone a long time ago."

A quick grin came to Abernethy's lips when he glanced at Donahue. He said, "He don't think much of you, does he, Red?"

Donahue's face was a mask of murderous rage. "I don't think much of him, neither. We've palavered long enough. This is the time I've been waiting for. I'm gonna kill you, Cotton."

"You said that before," Cotton said wearily. "June and Fred Flagg are both alive. Without the FF, Broken Ring isn't much to sell to Abernethy, and it begins to look like he knows it. Killing me now won't help much one way or the other."

"So Flagg is still alive," Abernethy said. "Red, Harriman is a damned bungler. You'd better do the job yourself next time."

"Murder is a bad business, Abernethy," Cotton said, "even out here."

"If," Donahue added, "anybody knows about it, which they won't this time." There was the ominous click of Donahue's hammer being drawn back.

Chapter Eight

Murder on Broken Ring

THIS, COTTON THOUGHT, WAS IT. HE SAW DONAHUE'S LIPS come away from his dark teeth in a triumphal grin, saw the mocking glint in the man's green eyes, saw the knuckles of Donahue's trigger finger whiten as he tightened the squeeze. Red Donahue was drawing this out, enjoying the full anticipation of it.

"It takes a brave man to kill one who isn't heeled," Cotton taunted. "Give me my gun, Red, and a fair draw. Then it'll be a killing you can brag about."

"No use . . ." Donahue began.

Suddenly Abernethy seemed to make up his mind. "This isn't his day to die, Red. Put up your iron. Drennan, mount up and light out for Broken Ring. Malloy wants you."

"But damn it, Mitch . . ." Donahue stopped, eyes whipping to Abernethy's face as if he realized he'd made a mistake. Then he said stiffly, "Mr. Abernethy, you can't let him go. He knows about Luke Bray and his wife. He knows about the Flaggs. He knows that Malloy . . ."

"Some men never learn when to talk and when not to talk," Abernethy said sharply. "Put up your gun. Mount up, Drennan, and you might think about my offer."

Donahue cursed under his breath. For a moment he pinned his gaze on Abernethy's face. Then he slowly dropped his gun into leather, and strode toward the lava where he and Abernethy had hidden. Cotton stepped into the saddle, trying to read Abernethy's face, and was unable to do it. The impassive expression had gone. In its place was one of satisfaction; the sort of look a man might have when he has thought a problem through and has found an answer that suits him.

"My gun . . ." Cotton began.

"Go along," Abernethy snapped. "You will do without your gun."

Cotton went then, and did not look back. He had stood, a few minutes ago, the closest he had ever been to death, and he could not understand why he was alive. Long before he reached Broken Ring, he was convinced that J. Francis Abernethy was the most dangerous man of them all, but why Abernethy wanted him left alive Cotton could not guess. Somehow Abernethy must have thought of some way he could use Cotton, but the manner of that, too, was something Cotton could not see at the time. It was enough that he was alive, and he was thinking of Broken Ring and wondering what had happened there before he came within view of the ranch buildings.

One thing Jackson Malloy had done and done well, Cotton admitted to himself as he topped the ridge north of Broken Ring. Malloy had built what should become the greatest ranch in central Oregon. If J. Francis Abernethy was the man he claimed to be, and had the money he was supposed to have, this spread should be exactly the sort of thing the millionaire wanted. If the watering place on Flagg's FF could be bought, Broken Ring would have everything. It might be a little more reasonable, Cotton thought, if the FF absorbed Broken Ring instead of the other way around.

BUCKAROO'S CODE   73

Broken Ring's big ranch house was a pleasant place of stone and lodgepole logs surrounded by tall pines. Behind the house and to the north a large spring burst from the side of the hill, forming, for much of the year, a fair-sized creek that flowed westward to eventually reach White River. It was this spring that made Broken Ring, but in the summer it went nearly dry, running only enough water for the house and horses.

Cotton had not traveled fast after he had left Abernethy and Donahue, but he was surprised to see their horses racked in front of the ranch house. As Cotton stepped down, he saw his gun and belt hanging from the horn of Abernethy's saddle. He took it down, buckled the belt around him, and examined the gun. Apparently it had not been tampered with. He stood staring at it, trying to probe Abernethy's mind, and failing. The Easterner knew he would be here soon, yet the gun and belt had been left where he would immediately see them. The horses showed evidence of having been ridden hard. Abernethy wanted the gun back in Cotton's hand. Back on the ridge he had been afraid to let Cotton have it, so he had taken this means of giving it back, but why? For that question Cotton had no answer.

Cotton slipped the gun back into leather, and moved up the path to the house. Malloy, he judged, would be in his office, and Malloy might be able to answer some of the questions that were in Cotton's mind. The office was in the northwest corner of the house, and to reach it Cotton had to go through the front door and the length of the front room. Here, again, Jackson Malloy had done a good job. It was the sort of room a man like Abernethy would like. There was a great stone fireplace at one end. In the center of the room was a heavy table. A scattering of chairs was along the wall and around the table; most of them were covered by skins or Indian blankets. On the walls were hung a variety of guns, knives, and Indian weapons. It was, Cotton thought, a masterpiece created for one purpose only: to sell.

The door into Malloy's office was open, but Malloy was not there. A stirring of anxiety was in Cotton when he saw that the office was empty. He remembered Abernethy and Donahue had ridden hard to get here ahead of him, and it was possible that their purpose was to murder Malloy. Yet that seemed unlikely in view of the fact that Abernethy and Donahue had had time and opportunity before to kill Malloy if that was their purpose.

Cotton stood for a moment inside the office, noting the papers that were on the desk, the pen with ink upon it not yet dried, and the uncorked ink bottle. Obviously Malloy had been here very recently. Cotton pondered what might have taken him so suddenly from his desk, and the worry in him rose when he thought that Abernethy and Donahue could have come only within the last few minutes. Again Abernethy's strange actions with his gun came to his mind. For some reason the Easterner first wanted the gun in his possession, and then he wanted it back in Cotton's hands. Cotton drew the gun, ejected the loads, and stuffed new shells into the cylinder. He dropped the shells he had removed into his pocket, carefully examined the gun, and still could find nothing wrong.

Cotton left the house. If Malloy were dead, there was nothing Cotton could do on Broken Ring. He'd pick up his things, and join Santiam Jones and Bill Curry at Slow Spring. He'd go on to Nevada with them to get the cattle Sandra Taney had bought. After that, well, there were worse things than 'rodding Sandra Taney's spread.

Halfway to the bunkhouse Cotton paused, suddenly aware that the place seemed deserted. Usually someone was working around the barn. If it were Bud Kroft, he would be whistling. Or there would be the racket from the shop of someone clanging at the anvil. Or Red Donahue would be in a corral, loudly cursing a buckaroo or a horse. Cotton heard none of these thing now, nor did he see anyone. There was smoke rising from the kitchen chimney, and horses were in the pole corrals. Beyond that he could see no sign of life, and it

BUCKAROO'S CODE

bothered him. It was not right. A sharp feeling of uneasiness keened through Cotton as he wondered if Abernethy had let him live back there on the ridge only in order to kill him now for some strange, obscure reason.

No shot came from the gun of a hidden killer; no slug came tearing life from Cotton. He went on, seeing the senselessness of standing in the open with the sharp midday sun upon him. Then, stepping into the bunkhouse, he saw instantly what had happened. Keno Harriman, Butch Ramsay, Deuce Hinson, and the rest of the gun pack were standing or sitting along the east side of the bunkhouse. All of them were armed, but only Harriman had a gun in his hand. Across from them were the buckaroos: Al Rhyman, Bud Kroft, and the others. None of them carried guns. Never, in the year Cotton had spent on Broken Ring, had he seen the line between the two groups so clearly drawn.

"You're the devil to kill," Harriman said, his thin, hard face showing puzzlement. "It don't make no never mind now. Git over with the rest of them cow nurses. Take off your gun belt, and drop it yonder in the corner."

Cotton did not move. His eyes locked with Harriman's flinty ones; the smile on his face a cold, mirthless twist of his lips. "You figgered I'd be purty well cooked by now, didn't you, Keno? You've got a hard-case rep, but you're plumb yellow. Too yellow, I reckon, to stick that hogleg back where it belongs and smoke it out with me."

Harriman's eyes narrowed. "Don't talk too big, Cotton. Don't think 'cause you came back from hell once is any reason you'll go on living forever. I've got a bunch of things to settle with you, which same I aim to do soon as I get a free hand. Right now I've got orders. Git over there now like I said."

Still Cotton made no move. His eyes ranged contemptuously over the line of gunmen from Harriman to big-necked Butch Ramsay on the end. "I dunno," he breathed, "why God gave crawling things like you sidewinders two legs, and let you look like humans. You sure as hell give an awful stink to the whole breed. Take Luke Bray and his wife. Take the Flaggs. Take Toad Maxon, who tried to 'bush me in town the other night. Why, I'd rather stand here before a bunch of . . ."

Butch Ramsay squalled a curse, and yanked off his gun belt. "Shut up," he snarled. "We was told not to start no gunplay, but we wasn't told we couldn't beat hell out of a smart-aleck, long-tongued, sashay-dude like you. Get your gun belt off. I'm gonna fix that mug of yours so June Flagg won't know it."

"Why, Butch," Cotton mocked, "didn't you burn the Flagg cabin? What makes you think June is still alive? Mebbe you didn't kick around through the ashes and find her bones. Is that it?"

Ramsay came toward Cotton, great fists knotted, his wide, whisky-mottled face terrible in rage. "You gonna fight, or are you yaller?"

"Don't do it, Cotton," Al Rhyman cried. "You know what Butch is."

Cotton knew all right. Butch Ramsay had been known to kill a man with his fists in the Empress Saloon in Antioch. He was the best barroom fighter on White River, they said, and he knew all the rotten tricks of a man who does not care how he wins so long as he does. Yet, knowing that, Cotton took off his gun belt, and dropped it into the corner on top of the pile that belonged to the other buckaroos. Not once had the contemptuous grin left his face. He said, "I know, Al. I've seen this crawling thing do what he calls fighting. It's the same as tackling a baboon. All muscle and no brain. Someday, when he cashes in, I'm gonna take an ax, and open up that hunk o' bone we call a skull. Chances are there's no brain there. Just a mess o' meat."

Behind Al Rhyman a man tittered. There was no other sound. Harriman and the rest stood in utter silence, unable to understand why Cotton would keep on infuriating this man he was going to fight. Ramsay, too, stood still, his beady eyes on Cotton. He was cocked for trouble, but, being puzzled by Cotton's cold courage, made no move. They stood three feet apart,

BUCKAROO'S CODE

Cotton's flat-lipped grin showing his contempt for Ramsay, and Ramsay, torn between rage and amazement due to his failure to terrify Cotton, let his face show his indecision.

Cotton exploded into action without warning. He came in fast, drove a lightninglike fist full into Ramsay's face, ducked a sweeping uppercut, jarred Ramsay's belly with a sharp, breathtaking punch, and danced away around the table. Ramsay let out a bearlike growl, and went after Cotton. He cleared the corner of the table, and no more, for Cotton grabbed the table, and shoved it hard into Ramsay. Ramsay went flat, and as he fell, Cotton lifted the table, and smashed it down upon Ramsay's great body.

Behind Cotton a man swung a fist at him, hitting the back of his head. Cotton, without turning, lashed backward with his foot, struck the fellow on the shin with his boot heel, and stepped into the center of the room.

"No more of that," Harriman snapped. "Let Butch take care of him."

That surprised Cotton, but he didn't look back at Harriman. Ramsay had pawed the table away and was on his feet, wasting breath in a series of passionate oaths.

"Save your wind, Butch," Cotton taunted as he faded back before Ramsay's charge.

Cotton wheeled aside, sledged Ramsay on the side of the head as the big man went by. Ramsay turned about, and came at Cotton again, hand outstretched. Cotton stood still this time, and as Ramsay's great hands fastened upon Cotton's slim body, Cotton brought his knee up in a vicious, driving blow that caught Ramsay full in the face. The big man kept on going down, falling on his face as Cotton jerked away from his relaxed grip. Ramsay lay for a moment unmoving. A sigh went up from both groups of men then, the strange sigh of men who are seeing a drama enacted before their eyes that they cannot believe.

Slowly Ramsay raised himself on hands and knees, spit out a tooth and a mouthful of blood, shook his head in the manner of a man who sees the earth turning crazily before him, and came on up to his feet. He said nothing now: no threats and no curses. He advanced cautiously, as one who has learned his lesson. Cotton went back, circling the room, watching carefully for any sudden move from Ramsay, knowing he would have little chance if Ramsay ever fixed those great hands firmly upon him; yet he knew, too, he would have no chance of ending the fight by continually backing away.

Twice they circled the room. Then, without giving any sign of his intentions, Cotton reversed his tactics, and drove straight into Ramsay. For a time they stood close, slugging, no sound coming from them except their full, indrawn breaths and the thud of hard fist on bone and muscle. The need of this fight had been long in Cotton Drennan. All the hatred he felt for Harriman's crew was in the savage blows he gave Ramsay. In him was a sort of maniac urge to batter and smash, a murderous joy that came from giving to one man a small part of the punishment he deserved for the killing of Luke Bray and his wife.

Ramsay was hitting Cotton now, and hurting him. They were great, sweeping blows that had the jarring impact of an upsweeping club. Cotton took some on his elbows and shoulders, or rolled his head with others, or ducked to come in close so that he might drive a fist into Ramsay's face. Ramsay was taking a terrible beating. One eye was closed. His wide nose had been made wider, and it bled now in a steady stream. The left side of his mouth had been smashed and battered against his teeth. But despite the punishment he was giving Ramsay, Cotton knew his own strength was being sapped by the blows he was taking, and he realized he lacked the strength to put the bull-like Ramsay down to stay. At least yet.

Suddenly out of nowhere a fist caught Cotton, and sent him back in a turning fall. He wondered, in the weird, distorted second that it took him to go down, if this was the end. He knew what Ramsay would do once he had Cotton helpless before him. Cotton turned on over to his back, caught the blurred

BUCKAROO'S CODE   79

figure of Ramsay coming at him, glimpsed the great foot swinging toward his ribs. If he had been fully conscious, or had the time to think, he might have rolled away. Instead, and afterward he could never tell why, he rolled toward Ramsay, grabbed the foot to his chest, and brought Ramsay down in a smashing fall. The big man hit hard. Cotton had been hurt by Ramsay's kick, but not as badly as the fall had damaged Ramsay.

Cotton rose, waiting for Ramsay to get up, but when the big man was on his feet, he seemed unable to breathe. He stood there, almost out on his feet, mouth open in a dazed manner as he tried to suck air into his lungs. Cotton came in quickly, drove a fist into his already paralyzed belly, and sledged him neatly on the jaw. Ramsay went down, and this time he lay without movement.

A man beside Harriman cried out involuntarily as Cotton struck Ramsay that last blow. Cotton turned his eyes to them, looked at the frozen-faced Harriman, the knot-headed Deuce Hinson. They seemed to be moving up and down in a strange, distorted fashion. He thought, in a disjointed way, that he had put Ramsay down barely in time. He would not have lasted much longer.

It was Al Rhyman who broke the silence with, "That was it, Cotton. Give us our guns, Harriman. We'll send you all to hell just like Cotton put Ramsay to sleep."

Keno Harriman snarled an oath. "Shut up, Rhyman. There'll be no shooting now, I told you. We don't like you huckleberries no more than a little, but we ain't running this shebang. When we get the orders, you'll get your guns, and by hell, we'll beef every man jack of you."

Cotton tasted his own blood on his lips, felt his bruised face, and lurched out of the bunkhouse to the horse trough. He sloshed water over his face, took a long drink from the pipe, and buried his head in the water. As he raised his head he saw Abernethy coming from the house. Slowly reality came back to him. He made a step toward the bunkhouse, saw

80   WAYNE D. OVERHOLSER

Abernethy motion to him, and, not understanding, held his
ground. Abernethy came up to him. He stared a moment at
Cotton's battered face. Then he asked, "What happened?"

"I had trouble with Ramsay," Cotton answered.

A quick smile came to Abernethy's lips, and faded. He
wheeled toward the bunkhouse, and went in. Cotton followed.
Abernethy stood just inside the door, staring down at the still
unconcious Ramsay, and then raised his eyes to Harriman. He
asked, "What was this about, Keno?"

"Cotton came in talking big," Harriman said stolidly. "Butch
took off his belt and they went at it."

"There was no need of trouble, Keno," Abernethy said
coldly. "Not yet."

"You didn't tell us that, Mitch," Harriman said. "You just
said not to have no gunplay."

Cotton's head had cleared. He looked closely at Abernethy.
Two things had struck him as peculiar: one that it was Abernethy who had obviously given the orders to Harriman, the
other that Harriman called Abernethy "Mitch." Abernethy's
first initial was J. His middle name was Francis. Where, then,
did the name Mitch come from?

Abernethy had laid his eyes on Cotton. He said, "Malloy
wants to see you, Drennan. He's in his office."

Cotton nodded, and started to turn.

"Wait," Abernethy said. "Get your gun."

Cotton shrugged. "You'll have to talk to Harriman about
that. He's got an idea none of us buckaroos should have our
guns."

"Go ahead," Harriman said, "but if you try anything in here,
I'll cut you down."

"Pick it up," Abernethy said, "and go see Malloy. He's a
mite impatient."

It didn't make sense, Cotton thought, Abernethy wanting
him to take his gun. It didn't make any sense at all. There
was something here Cotton could not see. Some sort of a trick
was being rigged, but he couldn't see it. Anything, he thought,

BUCKAROO'S CODE   81

was better than being shot without a chance, and if he had his gun, there might be a chance. Without a word, he picked up his belt, and buckled it around him.

"This ain't got a good smell, Cotton," Al Rhyman said. "You'd better not go to the house."

"It smells like skunk all right," Cotton said, "but I want to see Malloy. I reckon I'd better go."

Cotton left the bunkhouse, but Abernethy did not follow him. That surprised Cotton. He wondered where Donahue was. The two horses were still in front of the house when Cotton went in. He moved the length of the room, saw Malloy sitting at his desk, and stepped into the office. In that instant a gun roared from the corner of the little room. Malloy slumped forward in his chair, head dropping to his desk.

Cotton plucked gun, whirling toward the corner as he drew. Red Donahue was standing there, a smoking Colt in his hand. He turned it on Cotton, and fired, but he was a split second slow, and his shot was wild. Cotton had dropped hammer. Donahue's body lurched with the impact of the slug, his face mirroring the utter amazement that was in him. His feet slipped out from under him. He sat down hard, head falling forward as his gun slipped from his fingers. Then he spilled over sideways.

Outside the office window Abernethy shouted, "Drennan murdered Malloy. Get him, boys."

Cotton went out of the room on the run. As he cleared the front door, he saw Abernethy chopping down on him, saw Harriman and his crew boil through the bunkhouse door. Cotton snapped a shot at Abernethy that dropped him belly flat, and drove him to cover, pitched two shots into the men in front of the bunkhouse that sent them scurrying inside. Then Cotton was in the saddle, and cracking the steel to his roan. He swept out of the ranch yard as bullets whined around him. Once he turned in his saddle and laced his last bullet through the bunkhouse door, the thought in him that he would be facing a murder charge as soon as Abernethy got to town.

Chapter Nine

"You Ain't Got a Chance, Cotton"

COTTON LEFT THE ROAD AND SWUNG EAST FOR MORE THAN a mile. Then, topping a ridge, he glanced back. There was a wild disorder of horses being saddled, of men running back and forth. Then Cotton was on the east side of the ridge, and thundering down it. He had a few minutes now when he would be out of sight from the ranch. Most of the country was flat, and dotted with junipers. There would be no shelter here, but another mile farther east was a dry canyon with steep walls fifty feet high. That was his one chance of escape.

Cotton put Redman into a hard run for the canyon. There would be a short interval of time before Harriman's men could swing into saddles, and get to the top of the ridge. If Cotton could reach the lip of the canyon before they saw him, the chances were good they would ride on toward town, thinking he would seek safety there.

Directly in front of Cotton the canyon wall held one break where a ledge slanted down toward the bottom. It was the only place for the space of a mile where a man could reach

BUCKAROO'S CODE 83

the canyon floor. Cotton reached the ledge, reined up, and glanced back. Harriman's men had not yet topped the ridge. Quickly Cotton dismounted and led his roan along the ledge until they were out of sight from the rim. There he waited. He reloaded his gun, and held it, watching the lip of the canyon above him. Minutes later he heard the beat of hoofs sweep toward him and go on past. Then Cotton led his horse to the bottom, mounted, and rode on.

It was only a matter of minutes until Harriman and his men would discover that Cotton had given them the slip, and they would turn back. Some of them would know about the ledge, and they would find his tracks, but he should have at least half an hour. A quarter of a mile from where Cotton had come down, the canyon twisted sharply to the north. Cotton followed it for five miles or more. There the walls were not so steep, and he brought his horse up out of it. He paused on the rim, eyes sweeping the juniper-clothed country. Far behind him he saw a cloudy rise of dust. It would be, he judged, just about where the ledge was. He smiled grimly as he turned his roan north, and rode directly toward Antioch.

Cotton reached the town at dusk, gave careful instructions to the stableman for the care of his roan. Redman had been ridden harder the last few days than he had ever been ridden in his life. Cotton knew if he had to make another hard run within the next few hours, he would need another horse.

Cotton left the stable, and went immediately to Big Nose Charlie's, where he ordered a steak. The restaurant man looked at him sharply. He asked, "I didn't figger you'd be back in town today. Looks like a buzz saw chased you back."

"You should see the buzz saw," Cotton said. "How about that steak?"

"Sure." Charlie nodded, and went back into the kitchen.

Thoughtfully Cotton drew tobacco and paper from his pocket, and built a smoke. This was the first moment he'd had to relax since he had sat here on this same stool early that morning. One thing was clear to him now. The man who called himself

J. Francis Abernethy was the real source of the trouble on White River range. How far back his influence went, Cotton could only guess. Luke Bray and his wife had been murdered before Abernethy had arrived in Antioch. After Abernethy had come, Toad Maxon had tried to bushwhack Cotton. The raid had been ordered on Flagg's FF. Donahue and Abernethy had stopped Cotton when he was on his way to Broken Ring, and, strangely enough, if it had not been for Abernethy, Donahue would have killed him. Now Malloy and Donahue were dead, and there was no guessing what Abernethy's next move would be.

Cotton mentally tabled the things he had learned. Abernethy had been called "Mitch" by both Donahue and Harriman. Donahue and Harriman both had obeyed Abernethy's orders, and with Donahue at least it had gone against his grain. Abernethy was familiar with a six-shooter, he was a cold-nerved, carefully calculating man who had stated flatly he did not make mistakes because he wouldn't be hurried, and he had offered Cotton a job.

One more thing Cotton thought he understood now. That was Abernethy's strange performance with the gun he had taken from Cotton. Apparently he had not been sure what to do with Cotton when he had been stopped on the ridge between the Dead Horse Hills and Broken Ring. Donahue had wanted to kill him, but Abernethy had seen a way to make use of their prisoner. He wanted to get rid of Malloy, and Malloy was too important a man to disappear without some explanation. More than that, Abernethy could not afford to have his murder blamed on Harriman or Donahue or any of the gun crew he wanted to use. So he had seen to it that Cotton had his gun, and he had carefully rigged the play in such a manner that Cotton could be blamed for the killing.

Big Nose Charlie came in with the steak, and slid it across the counter to Cotton. He asked curiously, "Who was the buzz saw you tangled with, Cotton?"

"Butch Ramsay," Cotton answered as he reached for the ketchup bottle.

BUCKAROO'S CODE   85

"You mean you licked him?" Charlie demanded. "Great, smoky hell-fire, son, you couldn't lick that galoot. I was in the Empress the night he tangled with that jigger from French Creek. He was bigger'n you, and Ramsay killed him. I never seen a meaner cuss in a ruckus than that ornery gink."

"He's mean enough," Cotton said, "but I licked him. You can believe it or not."

Big Nose Charlie went back into his kitchen, mumbling as he went. Cotton ate automatically, thinking again of what had happened at Broken Ring. He remembered how carefully Abernethy had made sure he had his gun, and how every man in the bunkhouse would swear he had taken it. Abernethy had not followed him, but apparently he had stood outside the window waiting for the grim drama to be enacted that had been so carefully planned.

Somewhere along the line the scheme had backfired. Certainly Abernethy would not have given Cotton the gun for the purpose of killing Donahue. Donahue had not feared Cotton. He could have shot Malloy a split second before he did. He could have turned his gun on Cotton sooner. His face had showed his surprise when Cotton's gun roared.

Suddenly Cotton saw it. Because of his cautious habits, he had checked his gun a second time; and for no particular reason, he had removed the loads from the gun, replacing them with shells taken from his belt. Now he drew one of the shells that had been in the gun from his pocket, and with his knife worked the bullet loose. THERE WAS NO POWDER IN THE SHELL! That, then, was the answer. Donahue had no fear of Cotton because he had thought the gun would not fire. Likely Donahue had planned to reload Cotton's gun with live shells, fire one or two, and claim they were the slugs that had killed Jackson Malloy.

A grim smile was on Cotton's lips when he had finished his steak. It had been a smart trick that had been spawned in either Donahue's or Abernethy's brain. With any other man than Cotton Drennan it would likely have worked. It had failed with Cotton because of years-old habit that had saved his life on many occasions just as it had this time. Because they had misjudged their man, Red Donahue had died, and they had been so disorganized by Cotton's surprising appearance from the house that they had been unable to prevent his escape.

"I got some raisin pie, Cotton," Big Nose Charlie said as he brought one from the kitchen. "Want a slab?"

"Sure," Cotton answered.

Charlie cut the pie, lifted one piece into a plate, and laid it in front of Cotton. He said, "You know that blond-headed gal who's been around town several days? Sandra Taney I think her name is."

"Yeah, sure, I've seen her."

Charles grinned knowingly. "They say she's been after you to 'rod the spread she's bent on starting. Gonna change your mind and take it?"

"Mebbe. What about her?"

Charlie didn't answer. Instead he said, "You don't reckon Malloy will let her get away with it, do you? All that Wishbone country is mighty fine summer range. I've been through there, and I don't remember many springs in them mountains. Seems like that Slow Spring she's taken from Santiam Jones is about the only one around. Malloy ain't the kind to sit still and let her have it, now is he?"

"Well, what about the girl?" Cotton demanded.

"Why, she lit out for Slow Spring this morning. Got Ed Buckles down at the stable to take some stuff out in a wagon. He started yesterday morning and ain't got back yet. I dunno." Charlie shook his head. "Ed didn't care for the job. No more than a little. He was afraid Malloy would burn a little powder in his direction when he found out what was happening, and by grab, I'll bet he will. Ed might not get back. I wouldn't have done it if it had been me. Damn a stubborn woman. You can't do a thing with 'em."

That, Cotton thought as he paid for his meal and moved to the door, was too true to be comical. He paused outside,

BUCKAROO'S CODE   87

looking carefully along the now dark street. It seemed deserted.
He wondered how much Donahue's death would change Abernethy's plans. He tried to put himself in Abernethy's place,
tried to figure out what the man's next move would be. Likely
Harriman had gone back to the ranch as soon as he had seen
that Cotton had given him the slip. The logical move, then,
would be for Abernethy to come to town and make his claim
that Cotton had murdered Malloy and Donahue. If Dib Alcott,
the town marshal, didn't pick him up in Antioch, probably
word would be sent north to the sheriff.

The smart thing for Cotton to do was to ride out of town
and keep on riding. Santiam Jones had told him that. So
had Doc Vance. He could not go then. Now he was in real
trouble, and he still could not go. He thought how swiftly
things had changed. Not many hours ago he had stood with
Santiam Jones and Bill Curry along the Empress bar. He had
told them he couldn't stomach Jackson Malloy and some day
he was going to have the supreme pleasure of taking a punch
at Red Donahue's jaw. Now both Malloy and Donahue were
dead, and in their place was this man who called himself
Abernethy.

At the moment Cotton did not know what he should do. If he
stayed in Antioch he would be arrested for Jackson Malloy's
murder. He was surprised Abernethy had not already come to
town for that purpose. If, on the other hand, he ran, it would
be an admission of guilt. Still undecided, he moved down the
board walk to Doc Vance's office, and went in.

The medico was sitting at his desk writing. He looked up
when he heard the door open. "Cotton," he exploded, "what
in thunder are you doing here? I thought I'd seen you alive
for the last time. Or maybe you didn't go to Broken Ring."

"I went all right," Cotton said, and stepped toward the
medico.

When the lamplight fell upon Cotton's face, Doc Vance
muttered an oath. "What happened?" he demanded. "While
you're talking, I'll see what I can do for you. You've got a

couple of places that don't look good."

"I've got more'n a couple of places that don't feel good," Cotton growled, "and plenty's happened. Jackson Malloy and Red Donahue are dead."

"The hell," Vance breathed incredulously, his dark eyes widening.

"What's more, this jigger who says he's J. Francis Abernethy is a plenty tough hombre, and he's playing his own crooked game. It don't seem like a millionaire would have to be up to so much devilment. I can't figger it, Doc."

"Let's have the yarn," Vance said.

Cotton told him what had happened. Then he said, "I can't just pull out now, Doc. That's all it would take to make folks think I really did kill Malloy, and with a big gun like Abernethy swearing he saw me pull the trigger, I'd stretch rope sure." He paused then, his mouth tightening. He added, "Besides, I've still got something to settle with Harriman which I haven't had just the right chance to get done."

"There you are," Doc said, stepping back. "Your face don't look quite so bad. You'd better leave them patches on for a spell. That one cut on your cheek is a mite deep. Get a little dirt into it, and you'll have yourself a scar that wouldn't be purty."

"Thanks, Doc. How's Fred?"

"Coming along all right. He's over in the hotel now. June's got the room next to him." Vance opened a desk drawer and took a cigar from it. Thoughtfully he bit off the end. Then he exploded. "Damn it, Cotton, you've got to get out. I told you that before. I don't see how one fellow can get into so much trouble. Ride fast and far and keep on riding. There's no sense of one buckaroo trying to bust an outfit like Harriman's. And this Abernethy, I dunno." Vance shook his head. "Something about that jigger that ain't right. I had a hunch right off the bat he wasn't no Eastern dude, but who the hell he is I sure don't know."

"I told you I'm not going, Doc," Cotton said roughly, and went out.

BUCKAROO'S CODE
89

Cotton angled across the street to the hotel, and asked for the number of June's room. He climbed the stairs, and moved slowly along the hall. He was not sure that he was doing right, but he knew he couldn't stay in town. If he did not come back, this would be his last look at June Flagg.

Cotton knocked on June's door. She opened it immediately, and stood in the doorway looking at him, a lovely, round-bodied girl who seemed to Cotton in that moment to hold all the things that were worth while to him in life. She was wearing a white dress that made her dark blue eyes almost black. She smiled faintly for him. Hope stirred in him then. He had never known a girl like June Flagg. For just a moment now the old closeness came again to them. He wanted to reach out and draw her to him and kiss her as he had that night which seemed so long ago. Then her smile faded. She seemed suddenly distant, to be pushing him away from her.

"I thought you'd like to know," Cotton said, "that Jackson Malloy and Red Donahue were shot and killed today."

"Oh!" It was a quick, indrawn breath.

"You have decided not to believe me," he said, his voice made rough by the dream that had been broken. "You'll have to decide again whether to think of me as a liar. I killed Donahue. I did not kill Malloy. I guess it's not important whether you believe that, but there's one thing that is. This hombre you danced with and called J. Francis Abernethy is not who you think he is. He's a coyote playing his own rotten game. I don't know what it is yet, but give him time and we'll know. If I'm guessing right, he'll be calling on Fred purty soon."

Then Cotton wheeled away from her, and strode down the hall. He'd had his look at June, and he had never seen her lovelier. Nor, he thought savagely, farther removed from him.

As Cotton left the hotel he saw a line of riders dismount in front of the Empress and go in. He stopped, drawing back into the darkness of an alleyhead, and watched. When they stepped into the lighted area before the windows of the saloon, he

90 WAYNE D. OVERHOLSER

saw that they were the buckaroos from Broken Ring. None of Harriman's men was with them, nor did he see any horses along the street that might be theirs. Then Cotton left the alley-head, and moved swiftly to the Empress.

They were all in the saloon, every man who had taken buckaroo pay from Malloy within the last six months except Santiam Jones and Bill Curry. None of them carried guns. Cotton came through the batwings and was almost to the bar before they knew he was there. It was Al Rhyman at the end of the line, his drink half-lifted, who heard someone coming, turned his head, and saw who it was.

"I'll be a sunovagun," Rhyman howled. "Wouldn't old Keno like to be here in my shoes right now!"

They gathered around Cotton, pounded him on the back, and shoved half a dozen drinks at him.

"Hold on to your tongues," Cotton begged, pushing away the drinks. "I want to know what happened."

"Well," Rhyman began, "after you plugged Donahue and Malloy . . ."

"Hold on again," Cotton broke in. "I shot Donahue all right, but I didn't get Malloy. Donahue got him as I came in."

They stared at him a moment in absolute silence. Then Bud Kroft asked, "What was that you said?"

"I said Donahue shot Malloy just as I came in."

"But why would he do that?" Rhyman demanded.

"Donahue and Malloy were on the outs. From what Malloy said, Donahue was blackmailing him. Otherwise he'd have got rid of Harriman's crowd a long time ago. Harriman was supposed to be taking orders from Malloy, but actually it was Donahue who was calling the turns. Malloy was figgering on giving me the ramrod job, and firing Donahue and the whole outfit. He knew it would be a fight, and it might get him a rope halter, but he said he'd taken all from Donahue he could."

"But Abernethy said . . ." Kroft began.

"I know," Cotton growled. "He's figgering on hanging me for Malloy's killing. It's a purty scheme. He saw that I got my

BUCKAROO'S CODE   91

gun so you'd all know I had it, but what you didn't know was that him and Donahue had stopped me and taken my gun. I didn't have it till I rode up in front of the house, and found it on his saddle. Later I changed loads, and found out that they'd taken the powder out of them." He dug a handful of cartridges from his pocket, and handed them to the buckaroos. "Donahue must have figgered on beefing me, claiming I beefed Malloy, and he could have claimed the credit of getting me just as I shot Malloy."

"This Abernethy says . . ." Kroft began again.

"Don't tell me what Abernethy says," Cotton roared." He's the biggest crook and the biggest liar between the Cascade Mountains and hell. He ain't no Eastern dude millionaire, but I sure don't know who or what he is. All I know is that he'll try to hang me for Malloy's killing, and I don't aim to let no such thing happen."

"He sure cussed Keno good for letting you get away," Rhyman said. "He was fit to be tied. He came into the bunk-house, and said he'd bought Broken Ring. He'd completed the deal just before you, I mean Red, shot Malloy. He claimed he wouldn't need us, that he had other men coming in, so he paid us off, and we lit a shuck out of there."

"Your guns?" Cotton asked.

Kroft laughed sourly. "He knew damned well we'd use 'em on Harriman's crowd, so he made us leave 'em there. Mebbe he had other ideas, like figgering they might need some extra irons if they had trouble."

"What are you gonna do now?" Cotton demanded.

"Get to hell out of here," Kroft growled. "I never owed nothing to Jackson Malloy. For my money he was a hell of a cowman. Anyhow he's dead. I'm riding for Harney valley. I'll get on with some of them big outfits there."

"Me, too," another buckaroo said.

Cotton looked around the circle of men. All of them but Al Rhyman were pulling out. Rhyman said, "I'm sticking, gents. I've got a feeling Broken Ring ain't gonna be Abernethy's long. Dunno why. Just a hunch. And I've got a hunch Cotton ain't hitting the trail."

"That's right," Cotton said. "I ain't decided what's the smart thing for me to do, but I ain't leaving the country and letting a murder charge hang over me."

"Hey, Cotton."

Cotton swung toward the batwings. Big Nose Charlie had burst through them, and stood there blowing hard as if he had been running.

"What's up?" Cotton asked.

Charlie pulled in a lungful of air. Then he panted, "Abernethy's in town. So's that gun-slinging outfit of Harriman's. They're sitting at the counter while their steaks cook. I shoved out the back so I could get over here. Don't tell 'em, or they'll kill me, but they're figgering on hanging you for Malloy's killing."

"I know," Cotton said evenly.

Charlie puffed a few seconds. Then he added, "Abernethy was asking where Fred Flagg is. When I told him Fred had been shot and was in the hotel, he pulled out. And Cotton, you hit the dirt. You won't have a chance with that damned bunch of killers."

Chapter Ten

Arrested

THEY STOOD THERE IN SILENCE FOR A LONG MINUTE, BIG nose Charlie just inside the batwings, Cotton and the rest of the buckaroos at the bar. Then Bud Kroft let out a gusty sigh. He said, "I'm hungry, and it's a hell of a long ways to Harney valley, but I ain't hanging around here. I'm riding." Kroft strode out of the saloon, all the others following him but Al Rhyman.

When they had gone, and their hoofbeats had died eastward, Big Nose Charlie wiped his forehead. "I've got to get back. Sadie's got more'n she can handle. Don't tell 'em I came over here, Cotton. They'd just as soon plug me as not."

"Thanks, Charlie," Cotton said. "I won't tell 'em. Was Ramsay with 'em?"

A quick smile broke across the restaurant man's craggy face. "Yeah, and he sure looked like he'd met up with two buzz saws. See you later, Cotton." Charlie wheeled out of the saloon.

"Well, son, what you gonna do?" Rhyman asked. "You can't stay here and fight that outfit. Too many. I don't even know where I could get a gun right now to side you."

"No need of you getting into it," Cotton said huskily. "I'll dodge 'em and ride out of town. We've got to wait till Abernethy shows his hand a little more before we can do anything. The thing I'm worrying about is Fred Flagg. Harriman thought he'd murdered Fred and June. Now Abernethy knows Fred's alive. There's a good chance some of Harriman's toughs will try to finish the job."

"You trying to say I oughta keep an eye out for Fred?" Rhyman asked.

"You do what you've got to do, Al," Cotton said. He poured himself a drink, and stood for a moment thoughtfully watching the amber shine of it, a leggy man with the lamplight falling full upon his bronzed face and showing the worry that was in him. They he downed his drink, and lifted his gray eyes to Rhyman. "Funny thing what makes a man do what he does. With Harriman and that outfit he's collected it's money and nothing more. I reckon it's the same with Abernethy. I ain't real sure. All I know is that he's a mighty cool, tough customer who figgers things down to a gnat's eyebrow. He thinks he's holding a pat hand, and mebbe he is."

"With us," Rhyman observed, "it ain't money. That's a cinch."

"No," Cotton agreed. "Was I you, I reckon I'd ride on with Kroft and the rest of 'em. With me it's different. I couldn't pull out now no more'n I could fly. Every man has his own way of living. There's a right of things, and a wrong. Now Malloy had a little of both, and he finally got himself to a place where he couldn't work himself out without riding off and leaving everything he had."

"And Malloy wasn't a man to do that," Rhyman agreed. "I guess I'd never thought of it quite that way, but a man can't run out and leave the fighting to someone else. Not if he's

BUCKAROO'S CODE 95

gonna look at himself any more and not hate the sight of his own face."

"That's right. I'd like to live here. I'd like to be a part of this country when it grows up." Cotton gestured wearily. "I'd like to be here fifty years from now to attend an old-timers' convention, and tell 'em what I'd done to make this a good country. Trouble is it won't be a good country long as a big outfit like Broken Ring is in the hands of a man who don't think of nothing but his own dirty scheming. Abernethy's gonna claim Broken Ring. That's the way I've got it pegged, and who's gonna stop him?"

"He's already claiming it," Rhyman said quickly. "We told you that. Said he'd bought the spread from Malloy. I dunno how he's gonna make it stick, but that's what he said."

"He's got a damned good idea how he's gonna make it stick," Cotton said, "or he wouldn't be making no claim like that."

"You'd better light a shuck out of here," Rhyman said uneasily. "They're gonna be full of grub purty soon, and they'll mosey in here. Then it'll be up to you to swap lead with the whole outfit."

"I'm going up to the hotel. Trouble is June can't seem to make up her mind whether I'm on the square or not. Now mebbe she'll believe you, Al. The one big thing to get through her head is that Abernethy can't be trusted no more than any sidewinder. I don't know what shape Fred's in. If he can't talk, Abernethy will try to do business with June. Or he might be smart enough to let the thing slide for a while."

"I'll see June," Rhyman said. "Now git. Go out through the back. They'll hear you're in town, and they'll comb the place till they root you out."

Cotton grinned. "I'll go dig myself a hole and climb in, Al. See you later," and went out through the back into the alley.

Cotton was surprised that Harriman and his men had not started a hunt for him already. They must have heard he was in town. He stood for a moment looking along the alley, and seeing no one, strode to the corner and around it to the hotel. For a short moment he was in the light as he stepped into the lobby, but no shot came from the darkness, no yell to ring along the street that this was the man they sought. He strode rapidly across the lobby, up the stairs and along the hall, fingers close to gun butt, ears keen for any strange sound behind him.

The door to the room beyond June's was open, the lamplight falling through it making a yellow pattern on the hall floor. Cotton paused, heard Abernethy say smoothly, "I don't want to urge you tonight, Mr. Flagg. There is no need of wearing you out, and I certainly want to express my sincere sympathy for the attack upon your place. I cannot imagine who would do such a thing in this peaceful country."

"Peaceful," Doc Vance snorted. "What ever gave you the idea there was any peace on White River? You aren't in New York now, my friend."

"I am aware of that, Doctor. I still can see no reason why such a murderous attack should be made upon a peaceful settler like Mr. Flagg."

"I saw you ride into town with Harriman and his bunch of plug-uglies," Vance said dryly. "You might ask him."

"I will," Abernethy said sharply, "if you think he knows anything about it. Can you prove your intimation, Doctor?"

"Yeah, by the process of elimination. There isn't anybody else who would do a dirty stunt like that."

"That would hardly hold in a court of law. But there is no use to continue this discussion. Mr. Flagg, from what I have seen of the country, Broken Ring and your FF by nature were designed to be part and parcel of the same place. Now let's do it one way or the other. Either you buy me out, or you sell to me. You think it over, and decide which way it will be."

"I ain't got a nickel, Abernethy," Flagg croaked. "I told you that."

BUCKAROO'S CODE 97

"Then decide what you want for your property," Abernethy said briskly. "I would rather buy you out than to sell."

"I ain't selling, either. I told you that, too."

Cotton heard the scrape of a chair and steps as Abernethy moved toward the door. He said, "I am not like Malloy or his foreman, Donahue. I want nothing so much as to get along with my neighbors, but your position, Mr. Flagg, is hardly reasonable. Geography must be considered. I trust you will think it over carefully. Good evening."

Cotton stepped back, and stood in the middle of the hall. Abernethy didn't see him until he had cleared the door. Then he came to a sharp halt, surprise briefly running its path across his face, and dying.

"Howdy, Abernethy," Cotton drawled. "I'm sure glad to see you without that outfit of coyotes you're paying. Now mebbe we can decide right here and now whether there'll be peace on White River, or whether there'll be more killing and burnings like there have been. Fill your hand, Abernethy. We'll smoke it out right here."

"I beg your pardon," Abernethy said stiffly. "You are a murderer whose gun took life from Jackson Malloy and Red Donahue today. I would hardly be smart if I gave you a chance to do the same to me. Step aside, please."

"You sure lie, Abernethy, faster than my horse can run. You know damned well I didn't kill Malloy—which right now is neither here nor yonder. You're bent on following the same dirty pattern Red Donahue set. Now I got nothing to gain except the satisfaction of knowing I done a good job. And mebbe I'd have a chance to live here in a country I like with folks I like, and know there's gonna be a reasonable amount of peace. That's why I'm aiming to kill you, Abernethy. I said, fill your hand."

"I am not a fool, Drennan," Abernethy snapped. "You should know that by now. The town marshal will arrest you, and you will hang for Jackson Malloy's murder. You will hang because I will be there to testify that I saw you pull the trigger. It would be an excellent thing if you could kill me now, wouldn't it? Then there would be nobody to tell the story of what happened. If you do kill me, you will have to shoot me in the back."

Abernethy stepped around Cotton then, and went on down the stairs. Cotton could only stare after him in blind fury, the knowledge hard in him that there was nothing he could do, and that within a matter of minutes Dib Alcott would be here to arrest him.

"You crazy, mule-headed idiot," Doc Vance sighed from the door of Fred Flagg's room. "Will you ever get out of town? Alcott will shove you into the calaboose, and before morning Harriman's gang will have you hanging from a limb."

"I'm going now, Doc," Cotton said. "Come along. I want to say something."

Cotton had one quick look into the room as he went by, saw Fred Flagg's white, gaunt face against the pillow, saw June sitting in a chair beside the bed. She raised a hand and motioned as if she wanted to see him, but he went on. There was nothing, he thought, that they could say to each other now. She had had her chance earlier that evening. Now he would not see her again if he could help it until this thing was settled one way or the other. If he lived, and Broken Ring was in other hands, then it would be another matter. Hope, he thought grimly, dies hard in a man.

"You got in a hurry at last," Doc Vance panted as he half ran to keep up with Cotton. "Where you going, son?"

"Thought I'd head for the Wishbones," Cotton answered. They went down the back stairs, and paused in the alley. "I know that country purty well. Better than Harriman. I figger Abernethy will hang himself eventually if we give him time and rope enough. All I'm wanting to do now is to keep him from hanging me."

"That's right," Vance agreed. "I'm glad you're getting some sense. I was afraid you'd want to stay in town and smoke it out."

BUCKAROO'S CODE

"I would if I thought it would settle anything, but I couldn't get Abernethy into a gun ruckus. You heard what he said in the hall back there. If I was Harriman, I'd have shot him in the back, only I'm not Harriman."

"What was it you wanted to say?" Vance asked.

"Al Rhyman is staying in town. The rest of the Broken Ring buckaroos are riding on. I don't think Fred will sell out to Abernethy, and Abernethy is just as bound to get the FF as Malloy ever was. In fact, I've got a hunch it was Abernethy that ordered that attack on the FF, instead of Donahue as I had it figgered."

"That's probably right enough," Vance said. "I can't figure Abernethy out. He talks like what he says he is, and all that, but it just doesn't make sense. Underneath that smooth front of his I have a feeling he's as hard and tough as they come."

"I've seen a little of it," Cotton said. "Now that's what I'm getting at. If Fred hangs tough, which I figger he will, and mebbe goes back to the FF when he's able, there'll be the same thing over again, and next time him and June won't be so lucky. You talk to him, Doc. And move him some place if you can where Abernethy's outfit can't find him. They might even try shooting him from the window."

"I'd thought of that. I'll see what I can do. That all you wanted?"

"Yeah. I'm going down to the stable and get a horse. That Redman critter of mine is about played out. I dunno if Ed Buckles has a horse he'll let me have or not. Might be a long time before I get back."

"I'll go along with you," Vance said. "He's got some good animals there."

They went along the alley to the horse corral behind the stable. A lantern hanging from an upright threw its small light into the darkness. Cotton moved around it along the back wall of the stable, went in, and kept on along the drive until he found Ed Buckles. The stableman stared at him in surprise, and began backing away.

"Now I don't want no trouble, Cotton," Buckles said hoarsely. He was a small man with long, yellow eyes and a weak-lipped mouth under a bristle- sharp mustache. "Dib Alcott's looking for you. If he finds you here, there'll be trouble."

"I'm looking for no trouble with Dib," Cotton said sharply. "All I want is a horse to get out of town for a spell. My roan is purty well done up. What have you got for me?"

"I couldn't let you have a horse," Buckles said. "No telling when you'd get back. Mebbe never. I can't afford to lose a horse."

"I'm leaving Redman," Cotton pointed out, "and he's better than anything you own."

"Can't do it," Buckles said doggedly, and backed away.

"You took Sandra Taney's stuff out to her, didn't you, Ed?" Cotton asked.

"Yeah." Relief spread across Buckles' face when he saw that Cotton wasn't going to press the matter of a horse. "Just got back. Hell of a long trip down there to Slow Spring. Left here yesterday morning. Santiam Jones and Bill Curry have been working down there. They got things fixed up purty good. They cleaned out the cabin, and built a lean-to for the gal's bedroom." Buckles' yellow eyes narrowed. "I hear you killed Malloy."

"That's one of Abernethy's damned lies," Cotton said hotly. "Donahue killed Malloy. That was when I stepped in. I shot a little faster and straighter than Red. I got him all right."

Buckles cleared his throat. "I ain't shedding no tears over either Malloy or Donahue. I was plumb scared taking that load in for the Taney gal. I figgered Malloy or Donahue would run her out and plug me to boot. Now this Abernethy seems to be a little different. Mebbe he won't bother the gal."

"Don't count on that. When are Santiam and Bill gonna leave to get them cows Sandra bought?"

"In the morning. She's got a lot of plans, that Taney gal has. When I talked to her, she seemed more interested in licking Malloy than in starting a spread."

BUCKAROO'S CODE
101

"That so?" Cotton asked. "Well, Ed, I'm leaving town, and I'm taking a horse. Do you let me have it, or do I take it, and add horse stealing to my list of crimes?"

"You'll add horse stealing," Buckles snapped, and backed up another step, fear putting its mark again upon his face. "Dib would kill me if I let you have a horse."

Cotton glanced at Vance. "What you think, Doc? If I take a horse, I reckon anybody would have a reason to put a rope on me."

Vance muttered an oath. He growled, "You're an old woman, Ed. I'll pay for the damned horse if Cotton don't bring him back."

Buckles shook his head. "I tell you I can't do it. Dib would kill me."

"Hoist 'em, Cotton." It was Dib Alcott's voice speaking from the horse corral. "I wouldn't want to hurt you, Cotton, but if you make a fast move of any kind I'll have to drill you. I'm arresting you for the murder of Jackson Malloy."

Silence then, while Cotton's hands came slowly up. As he turned Keno Harriman's gravelly laugh sawed into the quiet. "You sure told the truth, Ed, about letting him have that horse. I'd have killed you if Dib didn't. This here's a dangerous man Dib's arresting, and the sooner we get him strung up the better for all of us."

Chapter Eleven
Pine Box to Freedom

COTTON TOOK ONE STEP AND MADE A TURN SO THAT HE FACED Dib Alcott and Keno Harriman. Both held guns. Harriman's thin, hard face was bright with triumph. Desire was plain to read in his flinty eyes. The slightest suspicious move on Cotton's part would bring a bullet from Harriman's gun. That Cotton saw plainly enough, but he saw, too, that it was different with Alcott. The marshal was a slow-moving, slow-thinking man whose brain could clutch solidly but one idea at a time. Never before in the years he had been the law in Antioch had he been faced with so much trouble. Now he was torn between his liking for Cotton and what seemed to be his duty. His eyes turned to the scornful medico, and came back to Cotton.

"I hate like hell to do this," Alcott said apologetically. "It ain't for me to say whether you killed Malloy, or whether you didn't. Abrenethy swears you done it, so I'm taking you over to the calaboose. We'll get word to the sheriff, and I'm hoping he'll come up and look things over."

BUCKAROO'S CODE   103

"It's quite a trip to the Columbia, Dib," Cotton murmured. "That star-toter down there don't like to ride much. Looks like I might be in your jug a long time."

"Not too long," Harriman said with evident satisfaction.

"None of that talk," Alcott said spiritedly. "We've never had nobody broke out of my jail, and I ain't gonna stand for it now."

Harriman shrugged, an evil grin on his mouth, and let it go at that.

"In case it interests you," Cotton said, "I didn't beef Malloy. It was a smart trick rigged up by this Abernethy gent. Him and Donahue took my gun away from me while I was riding to Broken Ring. Then they let me go on. When I got to the ranch, my gun was hanging on Abernethy's saddle. They had pulled the shells, spilled the powder, and put the bullets back, so Donahue didn't think I'd be doing any shooting. I had a fight with Ramsay, and I was washing up when Abernethy came out and said Malloy wanted me. He didn't come along. Just as I went into Malloy's office, Donahue let go at Malloy. I jerked my gun, and got Donahue. He was taking his time, thinking he had nothing to worry about from me. Abernethy was outside at the window. He let out a squall that I'd murdered Malloy. I hit a high lope out o' there, and managed to duck the wolf pack this dirty son put on my tail. Now if that's murder, Dib, you go ahead and arrest me."

Harriman snorted a contemptuous laugh. "It's a likely yarn, ain't it, marshal? He's lying right down the line."

"Dib, doesn't it strike you a little odd that Harriman here is such a hound to do things by law?" Doc Vance asked.

"I've got to arrest you, Cotton," Alcott said doggedly. "You tell your yarn in court. Now you'd better let your gun belt go 'cause I sure ain't hankering for trouble. All I want is to do my job, which same I don't like no more than a little."

"You go ahead and make a play," Harriman taunted. "I reckon it'd be plumb legal to shoot a man resisting arrest."

104   WAYNE D. OVERHOLSER

"So you're a deputy, are you, Keno?" Cotton asked. "The law is sure getting bad off if you are."

"I'll handle this, Harriman," Alcott snapped. "Put your iron up. I didn't ask him to come along, Cotton. He just invited himself. Now that gun belt. No use of you getting an idea about making a break 'cause it won't get you nothing but a slug."

"O.K., Dib," Cotton said slowly, but did not move.

Harriman had reluctantly holstered his gun. Cotton watched him, evaluating his chances of making a successful play, and finding them small in the face of Alcott's drawn gun, but they would be smaller once he was helplessly locked inside a cell. He thought he could count on Doc Vance backing him if he made a break. The medico had picked up a length of broken shovel handle from where it had been kicked against the wall. As he stood batting it against the palm of his hand, he said sourly, "I oughta crack you over the noggin with this, Dib. I never saw you make a bigger fool out of yourself."

"If you take chips in this I'll have you in the jug, too," Alcott threatened. "Now I'm asking you for the last time to take that belt off, Cotton. I never shot a man in my life when he was just standing there looking at me, but if you don't get a move on, that's what I'm gonna do."

Cotton had purposely played for time, and part of what he had hoped to gain had been accomplished. Ed Buckles, the stableman, had disappeared. Dib Alcott was proddy and impatient. One more thing Cotton needed; a weapon of some sort, and the only thing he had seen within any reasonable distance was a pitchfork leaning against the wall of the stall behind him.

"I sure hate to do this," Cotton said in an aggrieved tone as he stepped back toward the stall. "I figger a sixshooter is the only kind of protection a man can count on when he's bucking the sort of running mate you've got." He unbuckled the gun belt, let it fall, and again stepped back. "Dang it, Dib, I never

BUCKAROO'S CODE

thought you'd fix me like this in front of Keno Harriman."

"Nobody's gonna touch you long as you're in my jail," Alcott said sharply.

Harriman's grin widened, but he said nothing. As Alcott stepped forward to pick up the gun belt, Cotton casually reached for the pitchfork, brought it in front of him, and leaned upon it. He did not know whether Doc had caught on to what he had in mind or not. The medico was standing at Harriman's side, the length of shovel handle swinging carelessly at his side.

"Now step out in front of me," Alcott said tonelessly, "and head for the jail. Just keep your hands at your sides. I'm not taking no chances on searching you right now. You might have a hideout gun on you somewhere."

Cotton laughed shortly. "Somebody must have given me quite a build-up, Dib. You know I ain't half as tough a customer as you're making out."

"You're a heap tougher than I ever gave you credit for," Alcott said nervously. "Come on now."

"You're a hell of a lawman," Harriman said disgustedly. "He's just working for time, thinking mebbe somebody will show up and get the drop on you. Might happen, too. He's got some friends in town. I dunno why, but he has."

"Like me," Doc Vance said. "If I could get out of here and lay my hands on a gun right quick, I'd come back smoking it. Make no mistake about that. It wouldn't surprise me none if somebody like that little bowlegged Al Rhyman showed up."

"You ain't going nowhere, Doc," Alcott said, taking a nervous look behind him.

That one quick turn of Alcott's head was the chance Cotton had been waiting for, and he did not miss it. The points of the pitchford tangs were buried lightly in the litter of the stable floor. Now he brought it up in a quick move that caught Alcott completely off guard, tossing the litter squarely into Alcott's face, and for the moment half-blinding him. Alcott fired wildly over Cotton's head, dropping Cotton's gun belt and pawing at his face with his left hand.

Cotton's one chance of success depended on the medico taking Harriman out of the fight. At the moment he did not have time to see what the medico was doing. He dropped the pitchfork, and dived at Alcott. They went over in a twisting pile of arms and legs, Alcott still half-blinded. He landed on the bottom, the full weight of Cotton's shoulder hitting him in the chest and driving the wind from him. He pawed at Cotton's face feebly, trying to slip out from under Cotton, and was unable to do so.

Cotton rose, grabbed Alcott by the front of his shirt, and hauled him to his feet. He smashed the marshal full on the jaw with a savage, turning fist, the crack of that blow ringing the length of the stable. When he relinquished his hold, Alcott sank back into an inert heap. Cotton picked Alcott's gun up from the floor, and whirled to face Harriman, but the gun boss was in no shape to make trouble. He was lying flat on his back, out cold. A faint trickle of blood showed on his forehead. Doc Vance stood over him, twirling the broken length of shovel handle in his hand.

"Got him first crack," Vance said, grinning broadly. "He didn't even kick. Had his gun clear, and was chopping down on you when I let him have it. Reckon he didn't think I had it in me."

"Thanks, Doc," Cotton said hoarsely. "Now you've got yourself into it plumb up to your neck. You shouldn't have done it."

"Why not?" Vance demanded. "You think I was going to stand around while they stuck you in jail so Harriman and his bunch could hang you from a juniper limb? Not much. I'm a citizen as well as a doctor, and I aim to work at it."

"Then we'd best be riding out of town."

"Not me. I reckon I'm one man in this town even Keno Harriman wouldn't touch, seeing as I'm the only doctor within a hundred miles or more. Come on. That shot'll bring the rest of 'em in here pronto."

They were out of the stable before anybody came in. They stumbled along through the dark alley, and reached the barn that stood behind the medico's office. Vance was a bachelor who lived in a single room in the back of his office, and kept a saddle horse and team and buckboard in the barn. He said, "Cotton, soon as Harriman comes around, and maybe sooner, they'll post a guard all over town. Fact is, they'll probably dump the town upside down to find you. The thing we don't want now is a shoot-out. We want Abernethy to go on till folks get him pegged right. Then when we get a showdown, we'll have some backing. That right?"

"Right," Cotton agreed, "but this isn't getting anywhere at all. I haven't got a horse yet."

"You will," Vance said dryly. He opened the barn door, and stepped inside. He scratched a match on the wall, and lighted a lantern. "Help me get this team hitched up. I've got a theory that may work. Toad Maxon's carcass is still in the house. I didn't know what to do with it, so I kept it. Today I got word that some folks up on French Creek are cousins of his, and I'm to take the carrion up there. Now my idea is to stick you in the coffin, and get out of town."

"I can't ride no coffin into the Wishbones," Cotton said grimly.

"All I want is to get you out of town," Vance snapped. After the team was hooked up to the wagon, he said, "Now let's got get the coffin. Somebody'll be along pretty damned quick." He raised the chimney of the lantern, blew the flame out, and stepped from the barn, Cotton behind him.

For a short interval they stood listening. Hearing nothing that sounded suspicious, they moved on to the medico's house bulking darkly before them. "It'll take a little time for Harriman to get around to thinking straight," Vance said, chuckling softly. "Or if it's Abernethy who takes over, it'll be some time before he gets it figured out. Maybe it'll be time enough."

Vance unlocked his back door, lighted a lamp, and led the way into the room that he used for a morgue. Maxon's body still lay on a table.

"Grab hold of this box. We'll lug it out to the wagon."

Vance blew out the lamp, and as they carried the coffin to the wagon, he said, "I thought some of coming back after that black, but I might have to do some tall talking. Better just take him along. Now we'll slide this thing right on the wagon, and you hop in. The lid don't fit very good, so reckon you'll get plenty of air. Some day you'll be in a box like this to stay, but this time you'll just have a ride."

Vance lifted the lid, and after Cotton had lain down inside, the medico replaced the lid. He went back into the barn, returning a few minutes later with his black saddler.

"What is all this, Doc?" a man demanded.

"Oh, hello, Deuce," Vance said easily. "What is this? Why, it isn't anything at all. I'm merely going about my business, which is no concern of yours."

Cotton thought if it had been Harriman or Ramsay or some of the others the fat would be in the fire, but Hinson was a slow- thinking man, and Cotton wasn't worried about what would happen. Then suddenly he was worried, for Hinson asked, "What's in that box?"

Cotton drew his gun and held it over his stomach. He heard the medico say, "In that coffin is your old pal, Toad Maxon. He got mixed up with the wrong people, Deuce, and tried to kill a man. You know what happened? Well, sir, he got plugged, and he's awful dead. Now maybe you ought to go off and think by yourself."

"Yeah. What'd I think, Doc?"

"You might think how it would feel to die. Wouldn't be much doubt which place you'd go, would there, Deuce? Just consider spending eternity in hell along with hombres like Butch Ramsay. Or take Toad here. Wonder what he'd tell you if he could talk to you from hell?"

"Why, I dunno."

"I've got a hunch he'd say to get away from Harriman's outfit, and start living like a white man. You just go ahead living the way you are, and pretty soon you'll be down there with Toad, and you can hear what he's got to say. Well, so long, Deuce. I've got to be rolling. They want to bury this carrion tomorrow, I reckon."

As Vance stepped up to the seat and picked up the lines, Hinson said, "Say, we found Keno and Dib Alcott down in the stable a little while ago. They both was out cold. Abernethy figgered they'd got hold of Cotton Drennan. You seen him lately?"

"Well, now," Doc said thoughtfully, "seems like I did see him a while ago. He was over in the Empress, wasn't he?"

"Now, he might have been," Hinson agreed. "I'll go take a look."

"Oh, Deuce, what did Dib want with Cotton?"

"Hadn't you heard?" Hinson demanded. "He killed Jackson Malloy. We chased him a while, but he gave us the slip. I don't know yet how he did it, but we'll git him. You can count on that, and he'll find out he's bought himself a rope halter. You'll see."

"I'm sorry to hear that," Vance said, "I always thought Cotton was a pretty good boy. Well, so long, Deuce."

The medico drove away then, and drew up as Hinson called, "Hey, wait a minute. What's the idea of taking that saddle horse along?"

Vance turned in his seat. "Well, sir, Deuce, it's a funny thing. Ever been up there on French Creek?"

"No. Never have."

"You wouldn't believe it, but that's the damnedest, stickiest gumbo up there I ever did see. Never can tell when a man's going to mire his wagon and have to ride for help. Now, I sure do hate to walk through gumbo when it's wet. Ever do that, Deuce?"

"No, never did."

"It sure is a fright. Balls up on your feet something awful. It'd mire a snipe. I've had a few tough times up there, so I just decided to see that I wouldn't get caught short next time. That's why I always take the black along just in case a bad rain comes up. Well, see you later, Deuce."

This time when Vance drove off Hinson did not call to him. Instead he sat in his saddle looking up at the blue-black sky. He said aloud, "Funny gent, that sawbones. Ain't a cloud in the sky. Wonder why he thought it was going to rain?"

Chapter Twelve
Fugitive

AN HOUR AFTER DOC VANCE LEFT TOWN HE DREW UP, AND lifted the lid from the pine box. He asked, "How'd you like your ride, son?"

Cotton swung to the ground, and stood for a moment flexing his arm and leg muscles. "To be right honest with you, Doc," he answered, "that thing is a hell of a rig to ride in. Don't think I even want to ride to boot hill in one of them when I'm ready for it."

"You'd have been ready for boot hill if I hadn't got you out of town," the medico said as he untied the black. "Hear me talk to Deuce Hinson?"

"Yeah." Cotton chuckled. "I'll bet the next time it rains he'll ride up to French Creek just to see how bad that gumbo is." Then he sobered. "Look, Doc. You've got to go back after Maxon's carcass now. If Abernethy or Harriman spot you, you're gonna have a tough time explaining things."

"I'll explain a few things all right," Vance said grimly. "They won't bother me. They have to have a sawbones, and

I'm it. Maybe Abernethy will try to get tough, and maybe he won't. He won't get any tougher than his tongue can make him, and it isn't words that hurt a man."

Cotton stepped into the saddle, and sat looking down at the little medico. He said, "I hope you're calling it right, Doc. I'd never forgive myself if anything happened to you because of what you've done for me."

"Forget it," Vance said briskly. "I haven't done this just because I like you, Cotton. There's more to it than that. It's a principle, I guess. It's the proposition of a free people living in a free land. You've shown yourself the damnedest fighter between the Cascades and the Snake River. The way I see it, you're the one who can lick this thing because you can lead the fight and folks will follow you as soon as they find out what's going on. Your job is to stay on the dodge till Abernethy's game develops. Drop in on that Taney gal. I hear she's planning on staying in the cabin at Slow Spring. When I figure the sign is right for you to come back to town, I'll get word to her. Now vamose."

"I wish I knew how you'd make out when you go back," Cotton said worriedly. "Mebbe I oughta ride back to town with you and help you get Maxon's carcass."

Vance snorted. "That would sure be smart, wouldn't it? Say, I didn't think about getting you some grub, but I reckon the Taney gal will stake you to some bacon."

"I'll get along, Doc," Cotton said. "The country's full of deer. Or I'll drop over to the east side, and get me an antelope. So long."

"So long, son," Vance returned. "That's a good Winchester in the boot. If they get you cornered, you can count on putting a slug where you aim it. Now start riding, will you?"

"Thanks for everything, Doc. Mebbe I'll get this bronc back in good shape. If I don't, you can consider it a swap for Redman." Then Cotton turned his black from the wagon, and pointed him directly south.

By dawn Cotton had topped the Dead Horse Hills and had

BUCKAROO'S CODE

reached Bridger Butte. A chain of juniper-clad ridges ran southward to gradually lift into the Wishbones, and a short distance from where Cotton sat his saddle on the round summit of Bridger Butte the junipers gave way to pines. Eastward lay the desert with its sagebrush and bunchgrass. Out there in that desert, and not many miles from Cotton, was Sand Spring— and Luke Bray's homestead.

Cotton stepped down from the saddle and stood for a long time staring into the sunrise. Out there were the graves that held the bodies of Luke Bray and his wife, and Cotton thought of what June Flagg had said that night when they were in the cave under the burning FF cabin.

"It's strange how much trouble there is in life all because of greed." Those were the words June had used, and it was as true with Luke Bray and his wife as it was with Fred Flagg and June. June had said, too, "There was no reason why we should have been bothered. Dad never harmed anyone." Neither had the Brays, but they had both died, and the debt was not yet paid.

Cotton thought again, as he had so many times these last days, of his own father's death, and how he had come to look upon Luke Bray as a sort of foster father. The vivid image of the brush-covered graves, of the ashes where the cabin had once stood; all that again came into Cotton's mind with new sharpness. Yet, as he stood looking into the desert and the hills that were now brown and purple with the sun rising beyond them, a new thought came to him. If he could talk to Luke Bray, Luke would say not to go ahead with this fight for the purpose of revenging his and his wife's death.

There was another reason, Luke would say, why Abernethy and Harriman and the rest of them would have to die or be driven from the country. That reason was the right of those who were still alive, folks like Fred Flagg and June, like Sandra Taney, to make their living from this land. Someday there would be cities here, and mills to saw the pines, and dams on the river to raise the water so it would flow across the sandy soil. This Luke Bray had seen. He had said, "All we want is a chance to live here, Cotton. Run a few cows and a few horses. Mebbe the day will come when we can sink a well. Might even be you could save a stake, and come in with us."

That had been a dream. Now it would be nothing more, but there were those who still held dreams that would be crushed by flame and lead just as this other dream had been wiped away. Cotton turned to the west, saw the sharp, snow-draped peaks of the Cascades that were scarlet now with the early sun upon them. East of them ran White River, held between steep walls for so many miles, broken in the one place where Flagg's cabin had stood. That watering spot was the cause of this trouble. With it Abernethy would have everything he needed. Without it Broken Ring was only half a ranch.

Below Cotton were Broken Ring's ranch buildings. A thin column of smoke was rising from the kitchen chimney. Some-one was there, and Cotton gave thought to the idea of riding down to see who it was. Immediately he gave it up. Perhaps it was only the cook. Or again Harriman might have left some men there to take care of just such an opportunity. Cotton would be picked off before he could swing out of his saddle.

Cotton stepped again into the saddle, and rode southward along the ridge that ran, like a great, juniper-covered spine, into the Wishbones. Daylight had fully come now, fanning out into the canyons below Cotton. He smelled the sage and junipers and the dust; felt the strange, early morning brittleness in the air and the stillness that he had always noted in this high, mountain country. Once the stillness was broken by a buck bounding away into the junipers. Hunger was stirring in Cotton, but he dared not risk a shot here so close to Broken Ring.

Ahead of Cotton rose the high bluff of the mountain known as Wishbone Peak. He had never been to it, nor had he explored fully the country around it, but he knew Cold Creek had its origin somewhere near its base. Except for Slow Spring farther south, Cold Creek was the only water he knew about for

BUCKAROO'S CODE
115

miles around. He would find a hideout in the broken country surrounding Wishbone Peak. Later, when the hunt for him had died down, he would go on to Sandra Taney's cabin. That there would be a hunt for him he had no doubt. Neither Abernethy nor Harriman was the kind of man who would let him go easily. They held too much against him now, and the semblance of law was on their side.

Shortly after noon Cotton shot a buck. He dropped into the canyon that held Cold Creek, made camp, and cooked his meal. Twilight faded from the earth slowly, leaving behind it the deep silence of night and a star- burned sky. Cotton sat with his back to a pine, long legs to the fire, thinking of the night he had ridden to Flagg's FF, and the same thoughts came to him again. Why did he and Doc Vance and Al Rhyman and others live by the particular code they did? Why, too, did men like Bud Kroft and the other Broken Ring buckaroos look at life as if it were a game where they could keep on riding and dodge the issues that came before them? Then the other question, and the answer to this was the hardest of all to find, why did a man like Abernethy live as he did? Apparently he had everything he could ask for; yet this trouble was his doing.

Cotton thought back over the year he had been here, how he had disliked Red Donahue, had not respected Jackson Malloy, and how now they had both been dealt out of the game. J. Francis Abernethy had risen above them. Perhaps from the first he had been calling the plays in a manner unknown to Malloy. Even now, Cotton was not sure of Abernethy's game. Possibly he sought to steal the Broken Ring herd, and drive it across the desert to Lakeview and into into Nevada. Perhaps he planned to steal Broken Ring, and make a place for himself as a great cattle king in this raw country. The man might have any of a dozen schemes in mind.

Then, building a smoke, Cotton laughed silently at himself. Why should he try to call the cards before they were dealt? His job was to sit back until his hand was on the table before him, to stay alive long enough to play that hand. When he had finished his smoke, he tossed the stub into his small fire, and moved upstream above where he had picketed his horse. He bellied down and drank deeply. Then he stood up, listening. He thought he had heard the run of a horse on the ridge above him. He went quickly back to his fire, and kicked out the flame. Again he listened, and heard nothing. Every sound was a great racket in the silence, and Cotton laid to his imagination the noise he had thought he heard.

Again Cotton sat with his back to the log. He let himself think of June Flagg, but he found no satisfaction in the thinking. It held no promise; no hope. It was a forbidden happiness, of June Flagg and himself, a happiness that might have been attained if he had done differently. Yet, looking back, he saw no place where he could have done differently, nor could he put his finger exactly on the thing that had happened.

Suddenly Cotton stiffened. There was a sound this time. He could not definitely place it. Something was sliding down through the loose dirt of the north side of the canyon, and bringing a small avalanche with it. Cotton faded away from the coals of his fire, palmed his gun, and waited. He saw it then, a blur of motion above him coming directly down to where he stood.

Cotton made no move. He barely breathed; yet each intake of air sounded thunder-loud to him. This was no animal. On the other hand, it would certainly not be one of Harriman's gunmen. There was silence again, complete and disturbing, the sort of heavy silence that goes on through a seemingly endless span of time while two people wait, each holding himself rigidly, hoping the other will break. Then a soft voice called, "Cotton!"

Cotton's breath went out of him in a gusty sigh. It was Sandra Taney. He replaced his gun, and swore softly. "I'm here, and you're a fool. Do you know how close you came to being filled full of lead because I didn't know who it was?"

She came toward him, and when she was close, she said, "I realize it was a fool thing to do, but I thought you didn't

BUCKAROO'S CODE

know that two of Harriman's men are in these mountains. I don't know what happened after I left town, but I was at the spring when these men passed. Nobody has been in my cabin for so long that I guess they didn't think about looking. One of them said you'd head for town, and it was a loco idea for them to be hunting down here, that it was like trying to find a needle in a haystack."

"But you found me," Cotton said thoughtfully. "I reckon it wouldn't be so hard at that."

"That's right," Sandra agreed. "I've always had the feeling that until Jackson Malloy was dead, or his gunmen thinned out, I'd have trouble living here. I like it, and I aim to stay. From what I've heard the last few days, you're the man who might be able to do the job on Malloy. That's why I set out to look for you. I crossed horse tracks a few miles north of here. I thought I could follow them, but it got dark too soon."

"How did you get here?"

"I smelled the smoke of your fire, and from the direction you were taking I knew you were heading for water. I just kept coming, and almost slid into your fire."

"Where's your horse?"

"That was crazy, too," Sandra admitted. "I left him on the rim. I thought I could come down on foot and make less noise, but I guess I made as much racket as my horse would have. Now I've got to climb back up."

"If it had been someone else you might have been in trouble," Cotton said sharply. "I don't know what kind of country you came from, but some of the boys in these parts are a mite rough."

"I know that," Sandra admitted, "but I've always been able to take care of myself. I can now."

"You thought I couldn't?"

"I think any man could be killed from ambush no matter how tough or how fast with a gun he is. I'm selfish. I admit it. I've done everything I could to hire you, and you've said no. Still, I stand to gain what I want if Jackson Malloy is dead or ruined. I say you're the man, and so I'm going to do all I can to keep you alive."

"That's cold and to the point." Cotton laughed shortly. "I never have got you quite straight. You seem to be out to get Malloy."

"Right," Sandra said quickly. "From the time I saw you knock Red Donahue cold with one punch that night in the hotel dining room, I told myself you were the man I wanted to help me do a job of snake stomping. I haven't had much luck getting your help, but we're fighting the same enemy. It seems to me only common sense that we should be allies. Isn't that right?"

Cotton looked down at her face, a small oval in the darkness. He remembered the cool, calculating quality he had seen in this girl, the pride and the determination that was in her. She had set herself to swing him into her fight with Malloy. What was back of that fight and what was the real cause of her hatred for Malloy, Cotton did not know. Not knowing, he did not tell her of Malloy's death, nor of the other things that had happened. Instead he wondered how much of what she had told him now was the truth. He answered her question with, "I'm not sure we're on the same side, Sandra. You're fighting Malloy. I'm fighting Keno Harriman and the sidewinders that take his orders."

"It's the same, isn't it?" she demanded. "You're on the dodge because of Malloy, aren't you?"

"Partly, I reckon," he agreed. "Thanks for the warning."

"And Harriman takes Malloy's orders, doesn't he?"

"No."

Sandra looked at him sharply for a minute as if she did not understand. Then she demanded, "What are your plans?"

"Nothing at the moment," Cotton answered. "All I want to do is to stay ahead of Harriman's men. Doc Vance thinks we can close in purty soon, but not right now. That's why I'm here. I'll drop in on you occasionally to see if he's sent any word."

Buckaroo's Code

"I'll count on that," Sandra said, "and if I was you, I'd be a little more careful of my fire."

"Thanks," Cotton murmured, and watched her disappear into the darkness. For a long time he heard her climbing to the top of the canyon. Minutes later a horse moved downstream along the rim. One thing about Sandra Taney, he thought as he rolled up in his saddle blanket, was her great fund of determined courage. Whether she had lied to him or not, it took courage to ride at night in a wild country that was unfamiliar to her.

For a long time Cotton did not sleep. He thought of Sandra, and found that he had no clue to her trouble with Malloy. He thought back over what had happened the night before in Antioch, and wondered what had happened there that day. Some of the men in town were his friends, some were not, and most were those who felt neither friendship nor enmity. They were the ones who must be swung in against Abernethy if he were to be beaten.

Despite Sandra's warning, Cotton built a fire again in the morning, cooked his breakfast, then saddled, and rode to the north rim. He dismounted just before he reached the top, went the last sharp pitch on foot, and carefully looked out across the country. Seeing no one, he went back, mounted, and rode on to the top. He picked up Sandra's back trail, and within a few minutes knew that she had lied to him. She must have seen him coming, and watched him make camp along the creek. The sign showed she had kept her horse for some time above him along the canyon rim. That was how she had known who it was, and how she had been able to go directly to his camp.

Cotton rode upstream for a time, then dropped again to the creek, and watered his horse. He loitered there, still thinking of Sandra, and believing now she had not seen any of Harriman's men at all. If she would lie about how she had found him, she would lie about seeing the gunmen. He continued to ride up stream. This was farther into the mountains than he had ever been before, so he was surprised when he rounded a sharp twist in the canyon, and saw a high falls.

120   WAYNE D. OVERHOLSER

For a time Cotton sat motionless staring in admiration at the scene before him. It was like a long, white veil spreading wider as it fell. Curiosity stirred in Cotton. He had never heard anybody say where Cold Creek headed, and what sort of country it was around Wishbone Peak. It was too steep on both sides to get out of the canyon here below the falls, so he dropped back down to where the south wall could be climbed, and angled up the slope to the rim.

Because Cotton had no real thought that any of Harriman's men were within twenty miles of him, he did not show his usual caution, but rode over the last sharp rise at the top of the canyon, and almost ran into two of Harriman's gunslingers. One was a squat, tough man known as Stub Niles, the other slim and thin-faced with a sharp nose and chin. Cotton knew little about him except that he was called Pinch Gould.

Niles and Gould reined up in the same instant Cotton did, and in that instant fear showed itself on their faces. They sat motionless, watching Cotton, who was keeping his eyes closely upon them. A minute passed that way. Then two. Finally Cotton laughed derisively. "A couple of tough hands, ain't you, boys. Mebbe we'd better step down and make an even draw of it. Might as well smoke it out right here and now."

Courage of a sort had returned to Stub Niles. Slowly he shook his head. "Now, I don't see no use to make trouble out of it, Cotton. We've got nothing against you. Let's just keep riding in the direction we was going, and let it go."

Again Cotton's laugh jeered at them. "And get shot in the back? Stub, I know how you galoots work. I'm a little different. I like to be looking at a man's face when I smoke him down. If I don't get you now, I'll have to mebbe later when you're with Harriman and the rest of the wolf pack. This way I'll get both of you, and that cuts down the odds by two."

"You're a mite cocky, son," Stub Niles murmured. "Cocky and something of a fool. When you were doing your best, you was never fast enough to outdraw both of us because we . . ." The sentence remained unfinished, for his words had been for no other purpose than to cover his draw. His right hand swept gun from holster. He fired directly at Cotton, the thunderous blast mingling with the roar from Cotton's gun, and smashing apart the mountain silence.

Chapter Thirteen
A Woman's Hate

COTTON HAD BEEN NEITHER FOOLED NOR SURPRISED BY STUB
Niles's play. He had noted the lift of the man's right shoulder,
the slight turn of his body and the shifting of his weight. The
instant Niles's right hand started downward, Cotton brought
his gun from leather in a swift, rhythmical explosion of ener-
gy, and squeezed trigger. He never knew whether he fired
a scant fraction of a second before Niles, and ruined the
man's shot, or whether Niles hurried his draw so much he
was inaccurate. Whatever the cause, Niles missed, and Cotton
did not.

Niles folded, and slid out of his saddle, his horse plunging
away. Cotton whipped his gun toward Pinch Gould, but the
thin-faced rider was not made of the same stuff Stub Niles
had been. There had been the moment while Niles drew and
Cotton was lacing a bullet into him when Gould could have
taken one shot that need not have been hurried, but Gould had
no stomach for it. As he raised his hands, he called, "I ain't in
it, Cotton."

BUCKAROO'S CODE   123

Scorn was in Cotton when he said, "You're a yellow-bellied, crawling son, Pinch. You've got lots of guts when a man is on the run, but you don't have much when it comes to facing him and swapping lead."

"I don't get paid to die," Gould said sullenly. "There wasn't no sense in Stub doing what he did. Keno sent us up here to see if we could pick up any trace of you. He didn't say to do nothing else."

"Then you'd have high-tailed back to Broken Ring, and told Keno so he could have put the whole wolf pack on my tail. That right?"

"That's right," Gould said. He watched Cotton's face, saw the utter contempt that was in it, and fear became a naked thing upon his face. "What're you gonna do with me?"

"I dunno why I shouldn't put a slug into you like I did Stub," Cotton said. "Only difference is he had the guts to make a fight of it, and you started squealing."

"I got nothing against you," Gould whined. "You ain't the kind who'd shoot a man in cold blood."

"That's right," Cotton agreed sourly. "I never have, and I reckon I never will, but then I'm not sure you're a man. Got any proof, Gould, or are you a two-legged skunk who put on a pair of pants, forked a horse, and passed for a man?"

Gould reddened, but he would not be goaded into making a fight. Not even after Cotton had lowered his gun, and dropped it into leather.

"Well, then," Cotton said scornfully, "you go get Stub's horse, load Stub on it, and high-tail for Broken Ring. Tell Abernethy where I am, so he can bring the outfit in after me. Tell him mebbe I won't wait. I've been thinking I'd keep my eye on Broken Ring, and someday when they've all cleared out, I'll go in and burn the place up. See how he likes that idea, Gould." Cotton drew his Winchester from the boot. "Now go get that cayuse, and don't try to make a run for it, or I'll cut you down."

Gould bobbed his head, gigged his mount, and rode after Niles's horse. Later, when he had the body tied face down across the saddle, Cotton asked, "Was you in the outfit that killed Luke Bray and his wife?"

"No," Gould said quickly.

If Gould had answered otherwise Cotton would have shot him where he stood. Now Cotton thought he was lying, but he could not be sure. He said, "Mebbe you was in the bunch that burned Fred Flagg's cabin?"

"Yeah," Gould admitted, looking down at the ground, "but I didn't have nothing to do with burning it."

"You just went for the ride, I reckon," Cotton snorted. "Who did shoot Luke and his wife?"

"I dunno," Gould said doggedly. "Didn't even know they'd been killed."

That, too, was possible. It might have been a small party of only Harriman and one or two men like Butch Ramsay. Possibly Donahue had been along. Bill Curry had said Harriman's bunch rode by his and Santiam Jones's camp when they were at Bridger Butte. How many he might have meant when he said a bunch Cotton didn't know.

"Who is this jigger who calls himself J. Francis Abernethy?" Cotton asked.

"You know as much as I do," Gould said sullenly. "Says he's a brother of Pierce Abernethy, the railroad man. Says he wound up the deal for Broken Ring before you beefed Malloy. Claims he wants to make a big spread out of it, and he's got the dinero to do it."

"Soon as he takes care of a few other items like grabbing Flagg's FF and running me down. That right?"

Gould nodded. "I reckon them two are the first on the list. If you're smart you'll slope out of here, and keep on riding till you get to Mexico."

"Mebbe I ain't smart, Pinch," Cotton said. "Mebbe I'm so loco I'd hang around here till I get a chance to give Abernethy and Harriman and the rest of the sidewinders who murdered

Luke Bray and his wife what they've got coming." Cotton paused, his eyes narrowing. "One more question, Pinch. Who gives you and Ramsay and the rest of you your orders?"

"Harriman. Donahue always gave Harriman the orders. Now Abernethy tells Harriman what's up."

"And Malloy?"

Some of the fear had gone out of Gould now. He grinned when Cotton asked that question. "We all knowed Malloy was under Donahue's thumb, but we never knowed just what it was. Malloy was supposed to be running the outfit, and we kind o' pretended to listen, like the other day when we was all in town and you jumped Keno. Malloy said you was to be let alone, so Keno did some cussing, and pretended he was gonna do it. We all knew that most of the things we did was on Donahue's say-so, and not Malloy's."

"This Abernethy. You reckon he's had anything to do with the dirty business that's been going on?"

"I dunno," Gould answered. "Sometimes I think he ain't Abernethy no more'n I am. I've heard Keno and Donahue call him 'Mitch,' and once, quite a while ago, Donahue had me take a letter into Antioch that was going to a jigger named Mitch Ordway in Arizona. Now, I've allus had a hunch . . ." Gould's lips came together into a thin line, his eyes warily on Cotton. "I'm talking too damned much. You said you had one more question, and you've asked me three. You gonna let me travel?"

"Yeah," Cotton said. "Start moving."

"If Keno or Abernethy find out I've talked, I'll be a dead duck pronto."

"I don't have any ideas about hunting them hombres up, and telling 'em you've been spilling what you know," Cotton said dryly. "Now git."

Gould said nothing more. He reined his horse around, and leading Niles's mount, rode westward along the canyon rim. Cotton watched him until he dropped from sight. Then he turned his horse, and rode in the opposite direction. Suddenly

126   WAYNE D. OVERHOLSER

he pulled up, sat thinking for a time, staring back along the slope in the direction Pinch Gould had gone. Even if the rest of Harriman's crew was at Broken Ring, it would take some time before Gould could reach the ranch and come back with them.

Cotton turned the black, rode south and then west in a wide circle, and presently came to Sandra Taney's cabin at Slow Spring. She had seen him coming, and stood in the doorway, the morning sun falling brightly upon her. Cotton drew up, and sat looking down at her; noting the curve of her shoulders, the roundness of her breasts, the quick, warm smile she had for him. She was wearing a riding skirt, a tan jacket, and a wide-brimmed Stetson that hid most of her yellow-gold hair; yet above her loveliness Cotton felt the grim determination that was in her. There was a reason for the one, great, driving motive that was in Sandra Taney's life, and so far he had not found it.

"Mebbe you heard the shooting," Cotton said.

Sandra nodded. "I was getting ready to ride up and take a look."

"I ran into two of Harriman's men. I got one of 'em, and the other one decided he'd rather live a while. He's going back to Broken Ring, so it won't be long until we'll see the whole bunch."

"Do you think Malloy will be with them?"

Cotton saw desire in Sandra's eyes, and he remembered how Malloy had refused to talk about her. He asked bluntly, "What is it you want to do to Malloy?"

"Kill him," the girl said grimly. "Or break him."

"Why?"

For a moment Sandra did not speak. She met Cotton's eyes, the expression in her face that of a woman who is undecided whether to trust fully. Then she said, "Get down, and come in. The coffee pot is still warm."

Cotton stepped down, taking a quick look at the lean-to Santiam Jones and Bill Curry had built, at the spring and

BUCKAROO'S CODE 127

the small stream that rose from it. It was a nice place here, but it could not, according to Cotton's way of thinking, be developed into a large spread. There was too little water, hay would have to be brought from the meadows that lay west of the Wishbones, and the winters would be too severe in this altitude. He told Sandra that as she poured a cup of coffee and placed it before him.

"I know," she said. "I've been on a cattle ranch most of my life, but I'm going to break Jackson Malloy, and I think this will do. I'll take a quarter section on Cold Creek where there is plenty of water. Santiam says nobody uses the hay on the meadows below here. Malloy will not stand for it, but he can't fight a woman. What will he do?"

Cotton didn't answer the question. Instead he asked, "Why are you bent on destroying Malloy?"

"I'll tell you. I've done everything I could to swing you to my side. Everything except to tell you why Malloy does not deserve to live. I hope that will do what I have not been able to do." Sandra had poured herself a cup of coffee. Now she sat down across the table from Cotton. "I had a sister two years older than me. We looked alike, so much alike that most people thought we were twins. Dad had a ranch in Arizona not far from the border. If Jackson Malloy, as he calls himself now, had stayed away everything would have been all right. We had Apache trouble, and plenty of other kinds of trouble, but it was the kind of thing you could fight. You can't fight a woman's love for a man, Cotton, no matter how rotten that man might be."

Sandra got up, and moved to the door. For the first time since Cotton had known Sandra he saw her lose her cool self-control. Presently she swung back toward him, her face an expressionless mask. "Malloy had some money. He was a promoter, but he knew cattle and he knew what made a ranch. He talked big about his plans, and Sis fell in love with him. The upshot of it was she ran away with Malloy and got married in Tucson.

"I don't know exactly what sort of a mixup Malloy got into after they were married, but he was trying to develop some ranch property in northern Arizona, and he must have found out he didn't have the money to swing it. Anyhow, Sis wrote to Dad asking for whatever share of his property she would have when he died. He'd had heart trouble for years, and didn't expect to live long. He sold the ranch, and sent the money to Sis. Several months after that she wrote us that Malloy had left her.

"Dad almost died the night we got the letter. He swore he'd get Malloy. Then we heard that Malloy had shot a man, and was in jail waiting to be hung. That suited Dad fine. We went up north to get Sis, but she died the day before we got there. Maybe folks don't die of a broken heart, but I think she did. We were on our way back to Tucson when we heard Malloy had escaped. Dad took it on himself to chase Malloy down. He stayed on Malloy's trail for months, always a little too far behind to get his hands on him. There was a red-headed man traveling with Malloy that I think was Donahue, but I couldn't be sure.

"Then three years ago Dad lost Malloy completely. He had to hunt blind for a while, and it wasn't until a few weeks ago that we picked up the trail in the Dalles. Dad got sick, and died before he could come on up here."

Sandra tried to smile, and failed. She shook her head. "There it is, Cotton. I've taken a man's job. I'm here for no better reason than to give Jackson Malloy the punishment he deserves. I'm only sorry Dad didn't live long enough to do it. If I fail—" She gestured wearily. "Well, I'll never be able to look at myself again. I've got to square the debt, Cotton, and I need your help."

Cotton looked at this girl, dominated for so long by one grim motive, and he sensed the weariness that was in her. He said softly, "Sandra, I should have told you sooner, but I didn't know what was behind all this. I had you pegged a little wrong. Jackson Malloy is dead."

"Malloy . . . dead?" She stared at Cotton, eyes wide with doubt. "Are you sure?"

"I didn't stop and feel his pulse," Cotton said dryly, "but he sure went over like a dead man." He told her what had happened at Broken Ring, of Malloy's connection with Donahue, and of the accusation against him that he had killed Malloy. He finished with, "That's why I'm on the dodge. I've seen these things before. Mebbe the law don't amount to much in this country, but it's a good thing to have what there is on your side. Now I don't know who Abernethy really is, and he's a cagy galoot, but I've got a feeling that sooner or later he'll make a mistake. Then mebbe we can switch things around a little, and the law will be on the other side."

"Malloy dead," Sandra said as if she had only half heard what Cotton had told her. "Then there is nothing left for me. It's like riding to the end of a trail. I . . . I don't have anything to do. I came here just to bother Malloy. I thought I'd put him into a position where he'd attack a woman, and that would be too much, even here. All the money I've got is in the cattle Santiam and Bill went after."

"Then you've got the cattle," Cotton said bluntly, "and you've still got your plans for this place. Go ahead with it, and be thankful you didn't have to do the job of killing Malloy. Suppose you had pulled the trigger that killed him? You'd have had him in your dreams and in your thoughts, and you never could have got away from him. There would have been no value in it for you. Your sister would not have been brought back."

"You sound," Sandra said dully, "as if you had been through this yourself."

"Not exactly as you have, but I've seen what it does to a person. I've got the same problem on my hands. Luke Bray and his wife were murdered. I thought at first it might have been on Malloy's orders. Now I think it was Donahue, and maybe he was doing it for Abernethy. Before this is over, either I'll be dead, or they will. Mebbe both of us, but it isn't just for Luke

130   WAYNE D. OVERHOLSER

Bray and his wife. It's for other people who want a decent
living themselves. It's for people like you and Fred Flagg who
want nothing more than to be let alone to do their work and
get ahead. That's why men like Abernethy either have to die,
or be king. With him there is no halfway place to stop."

"I guess that's right," Sandra said. "Everything has changed
since I came to Antioch."

"No," Cotton corrected her. "It isn't that everything has
changed. It's simply that the persons have changed. When I
came back from Luke's place, I thought it was Malloy and
Donahue I was fighting. I didn't think of anything but squaring
up. Then I found out it wasn't Malloy at all. I thought it was
Donahue. That wasn't right, either. Donahue was just another
tough hand working for this Abernethy. He's the one, but I
didn't peg him right, and I still don't know how he got into
the ruckus." He paused, thinking of what Pinch Gould had
said, and asked, "Did you ever hear of a man named Mitch
Ordway?"

Sandra shook her head. "No. Why?"

"I just wondered," Cotton answered carelessly. "Another
thing I've been wondering about is why you lied to me last
night."

"Oh." Sandra reddened. "Why, I . . . All right. I'll tell you
how it was. I didn't see the two Harriman men, but I did find
their tracks, and I made a guess on a long chance that turned
out to be right. I knew you weren't a man who would run.
The Wishbones were the only place where you had a chance
to stay on the dodge, and still watch what was going on. So I
set out to hunt for you. I waited on top of the ridge north of
the canyon, and I saw you coming. I knew you'd hit for Cold
Creek because you'd need water, and if the tracks I had seen
were some of Harriman's men, which I know now they were,
I wanted to warn you."

"But you had no need to tell me the yarn you did," Cotton
said roughly.

"I know," Sandra said in sudden humility. "I guess I couldn't

BUCKAROO'S CODE   131

really make you understand, and maybe I didn't have a very
good reason. I thought if I told you I had really seen them, and
if I waited until it was dark, you'd . . . you'd . . ." She turned
away, and said nothing more.

"No, I don't altogether see, but that's water over the dam
now. I'll keep riding. One of these days I'll be back to see if
Doc got any word to you. And thanks for the coffee," Cotton
said, and went out. He mounted, and as he rode back into the
Wishbones, he turned his head, and saw Sandra standing in
the doorway. He lifted a hand to her, she waved to him, and
a moment later he had lost her in the pines.

It was well past noon when Cotton topped a high butte.
He reined up, and as he sat staring down into the meadow
far below him, he saw a long line of riders break out of the
pines, and come across the clearing at a brisk pace. It was
too far away to see who they were, but he guessed it would be
Keno Harriman in front. From the size of the outfit he judged
practically all of Harriman's bunch was there.

After Cotton had left Slow Spring, he had made a wide
circle southward, and had doubled back, hiding his tracks in
a sand-covered clearing. The wind would soon obliterate any
trace of his having been there. Now he was not sure whether
that had been the right move or not. Perhaps he should have
gone far back into the mountains, but again there was the lack
of water, and they would watch Cold Creek. A dull feeling of
failure rose in him as he watched them cross the meadow and
disappear again into the pines. Harriman would follow him as
long as he was alive. If he got Harriman, there would be Butch
Ramsay. If he stopped to fight them all, there could be but one
conclusion. There were too many of them. If he kept dodging
them, the chances were good he would run into an ambush.

Any way he looked at it, Cotton's best chances were to ride
higher into the mountains. It was not a good bet, but it was the
only one. Once more Cotton turned his black, and rode toward
the craggy top of Wishbone Peak.

Chapter Fourteen

Death Waits in the Pines

TWO HOURS AFTER COTTON LEFT THE BUTTE FROM WHOSE top he had seen the cavalcade cross the meadow, he had dropped down into Cold Creek Canyon. There he watered his horse, filled his canteen, drank his fill, and came again to the rim. He had lost valuable time, but it might be his last chance to get water for many hours.

Cotton rode around the falls to where the canyon flattened out, and drew up in sheer amazement. Before him, in an exquisite setting of pines below a high rim, was a lake. There was no wind, and its surface was like a great, blue floor. He had never heard of a lake being here, and he thought possibly he was the first white man to see it. Its existence was certainly not common knowledge on White River range, and he thought sourly how he had ridden down into the canyon for water, thinking it was the last he would find.

To Cotton's right rose the great pointed bluff that was Wishbone Peak. He thought of climbing it, and decided against it. It was better, he thought, to camp here for a time along the

BUCKAROO'S CODE

lake. Jack pines growing close to its edge afforded adequate cover. He rode along the south shore, shot a small buck, and made camp.

Harriman's men would likely come on above the falls, but there was no telling how soon. There was a chance they had heard his shot, or they might have picked up his tracks. Neither was a likely possibility, considering the distance they had to travel and the time that had passed. They would be more likely to spread out, and search carefully for fresh tracks. He could stay here and wait, or keep moving back into the mountains. He kicked out his fire as soon as he had eaten supper, and sat smoking, thinking about it. It was a case of hounds and rabbit, and the idea of playing rabbit didn't appeal to him. Always before he had been one of the hounds when he had been a player in a grim game like this.

Cotton stayed there that night, neither hearing now seeing anything of Harriman's men. In the morning he rode on, hiding his tracks for a tme in the shallow waters along the lake edge. Presently he left the lake, climbed a ridge and rode by a great flow of obsidian glittering like glass in the sunlight. Later he discovered a second lake farther east, and as he reined up and sat for a time staring out across its blue, wave-tipped surface, he wished for a fishing pole and line, and thought it a strange prank of nature that made him, a fugitive, the discoverer of these lakes. Eventually Harriman and the rest would be along, but the first sight of them had been his.

It might take a long time for Harriman to find Cotton, and here was as good a place as any to hole up. He rode on around the lake to a grass-covered meadow. There he put his horse on a picket pin, and made camp.

For a week Cotton remained along the lake shore. He had moved his camp to a sheltered spot on the north side where a bluff rose directly from the water. There was no sign of his pursuers until the afternoon of the eighth day, when he saw two riders come around the south side of the lake. One of them was Butch Ramsay. The other Cotton could not recognize at that distance. He watched them come warily as if expecting hot lead to greet them from the pines. Then they found the remains of his first campfire, and they sat their saddles for a time, looking down at the pile of ashes, and talking about it.

Quickly Cotton saddled, filled his canteen, and rode east from the lake until he was out of sight in the timber. Then he turned south. When it was dusk he made a cold camp. By going southwest he could skirt Wishbone Peak, and come close to Slow Spring. At least he would be in familiar country once he dropped down to the west slope, and he knew he would have little trouble finding the spring. It was time, he thought, that he found out whether Doc Vance had brought any word to Sandra.

The night was cold, but he dared not chance a fire. Ramsay and the other men would be behind him, and it was impossible to tell how close. There was the smell of winter in the wind that came down from Wishbone Peak. Snow would be coming soon, and he wondered somberly how long he could expect to play hide-and-seek with this bunch of gunslick killers.

Cotton was up before the sun, and again rode west. From one point he could look down into the desert east of him. It was like a great ocean extending far into space until it met the horizon. He saw a huge, semicircular rock that rose skyward out of the sand flat. Sand Spring and Luke Bray's homestead had been miles to the north, but this sight of the desert brought the full tide of memory back to Cotton, and with it was the grim knowledge that not far behind him were some of the men who had committed the two brutal murders.

The sun had cut away the last shadows of night, but the paralyzing mountain cold lingered. The grim thought was in Cotton that if he met up with any of Harriman's men now, he would be unable to get his gun out of leather fast enough to save his life. He rode on, still west, cutting slightly to the south to clear Wishbone Peak. It was almost noon when he stopped to blow the black that he looked behind, and saw four men break out of the jack pines, and cross an open space.

BUCKAROO'S CODE   135

Abernethy was in front, Harriman behind him. Cotton did not see the others long enough to recognize them.

The mountain, rising steeply before him, forbade a run. If it had been only Abernethy and Harriman, Cotton would have stood and fought, but four were too many. It was jack pine country here, much too open to cover a man and horse. Ahead of Cotton and to his right was half a mile or more of broken country, with an irregular pattern of steep lava upthrusts. There was his one chance, and slim as it was, he took it. He cut to the right, then up the mountain again, and rode between two sharp lifts of lava. There he left his black, and climbed to the top of the lava ridge that lay downhill from his horse.

For a time Cotton lost sight of the four men. He thought that they had not seen him, and they had been moving too fast to be following his tracks. If they had not seen Ramsay and his partner since the afternoon of the day before, they would not know his trail had been picked up. Patiently Cotton waited, gun palmed, bellied down atop the lava so that only the top of his Stetson and his eyes were visible.

Five minutes later they came again into view, riding directly toward where he lay. He smiled grimly as he watched them, wondering what they would think or do if they knew the man they sought was within a few yards of them. The other two men, he saw now, were Deuce Hinson and Pinch Gould.

Abernethy's high-boned face showed the savage anger that was in him. He was saying loudly, "I ought to go back to town, and beef that damned sawbones. Deuce, you're an incompetent idiot who deserves to have his heart cut out and thrown to the hounds."

Deuce Hinson's thin face reddened. "You've said that a hundred times. Why don't you just give me my time, and I'll ride on?"

"I still need you," Abernethy growled. "Now it's like hunting a needle in a strawstack. Mebbe he's holed up in a cave somewhere like that ice cave we was just in. We could ride within ten feet of him, and not know he was there."

At that moment Abernethy was directly below Cotton, so close that Cotton could have dropped a rock on his head. Gould had reined up, and Cotton had one bad moment, for Gould called, "Boss, a horse has been through here recent."

Abernethy pulled up his mount, and Cotton thought he was going to rein around. He did not, because Harriman said, "Hell, Pinch, that's Runt's tracks. I told him to go all over this country yesterday to find water."

The four of them sat their saddles for a moment staring at each other, the mountain stillness strained and brittle. Uneasiness was in them. It showed in their faces, but did not remain in Abernethy. He said sharply, "Keno, that galoot might be around here. Mebbe we'd better take a look at them tracks."

"No," Harriman snapped. "They're Runt's, I tell you. No use wasting time here. We've got one way to grab that hombre, and that's by watching the water. I say to go back to camp, and lay a string of men along Cold Creek."

"Yeah," Gould said, "only mebbe he's lit out for Broken Ring by now. He said he was gonna burn the spread out, Boss."

"He won't do that," Abernethy said coldly. "If we don't get him now, we'll pull off the men, and wait for winter to chase him out of these mountains. The way I've got him sized up, he's just mule-headed enough he won't run. Sooner or later he'll come into the open, and we'll nab him."

"Mebbe so," Harriman said, "only I like to pick my own fighting place, and this ain't it. We'll watch the creek, Mitch, and he'll show up."

"How about Slow Spring?" Gould demanded.

"Too much open country," Harriman snapped. "Besides, I reckon we gave that blond she-devil enough of a scare so she won't let Cotton come around. No, Cold Creek is the answer."

Abernethy scratched his square chin thoughtfully. "You know this business, Keno. I don't. There's just one thing I'm sure of. We've got to get this Drennan gent, and we've

BUCKAROO'S CODE   137

got to take his carcass into town for folks to see. That'll fix up Malloy's killing, and some of the hard-headed jayhoos like Fred Flagg will come down off their high horse when they find out Drennan's dead."

"Let's ride," Harriman said uneasily. "We're wasting time here."

After they had gone, Cotton held his position for an hour. He was sure that Harriman knew he was there. Probably the gun boss didn't realize he had sat and talked within Cotton's hearing, but he acted as if he knew Cotton was somewhere around. Obviously he had no stomach for a fight where Cotton was holed up, and they would have to root him out. What Harriman wanted was to wait him out until he was forced to come to water, and they would have him in the open. Cotton smiled grimly as he thought about it, realizing that Harriman might succeed exactly as he planned.

When Cotton left the lava he circled south. Harriman might have thought they had passed Cotton, believing they had him boxed between them and the mountain, and that he would come on later. If that had been Harriman's idea, he would have planted a gun trap somewhere ahead. It took hours for Cotton to make the swing, and the need for water was in both him and the black. He reached the summit, and dropped over to the west side, all the time wondering if he dared make a try for Cold Creek. There was no sense now of going to Slow Spring. He'd only get Sandra into trouble. If Abernethy had been up here in the mountains, Doc Vance would know nothing more than he had known when Cotton had left town.

Then, without warning, Cotton's mind was made up for him. Below, and riding toward him, were three men, one of them the swarthy gunman Harriman had called Runt. The two others were strangers, more gun dogs Abernethy had brought in, Cotton thought. He was in the open, and the country south was covered with jack pines and a layer of deadfall trees that would make fast riding impossible.

138   WAYNE D. OVERHOLSER

A shout rose toward him when they saw him. Runt had
jerked his Winchester from the boot, and laid a bullet close
to Cotton's head. Cotton whirled his horse to the right, and
drove home the steel. The black went up the slope toward
the rim of Cold Creek Canyon, Cotton thinking grimly that
he was bound for the canyon whether he liked it or not. The
chances were good that the four men he had seen earlier that
day were camped somewhere ahead of him.

This, Cotton saw, was the fight he had been trying to avoid,
but there was no avoiding it now. During the few short minutes
it took his black to reach the canyon rim his mind searched for
a way out, and found none.

Below him a shout rang out. It was Abernethy's voice.
"There he is, Keno. Get him, Pinch, Deuce."

Cotton whirled his horse to go up. The falls were not far
above him. Beyond them it was level on past the two lakes.
Runt and the two closing in from the south were firing steadily,
and dangerously close. The greater danger was below. Then he
remembered Ramsay and his partner. If they had not trailed
him, they might be close enough to hear the shooting, and
would box him in.

Quickly Cotton made up his mind. There was no use in more
running. Even with the odds as they stood now, a fight was
better. Cotton pulled the black to a dust-boiling stop, and put
him over the rim of the canyon. There luck was with him. He
had not gone far enough up to reach the sheer walls of the
canyon. Here the slope was gradual enough to give his horse
footing. Cotton jerked his Winchester free, left his horse, and
climbed back to the rim.

Cotton's sudden appearance was the last thing Harriman's
men had expected. They were closing in on two sides, naturally
supposing he had gone on down to the bottom of the canyon.
If he had, they could have picked him off from the top with
little danger to themselves. Now, without warning, Cotton's
Winchester began sounding its lethal message. Runt threw
back his head with the first shot, and went out of his saddle

BUCKAROO'S CODE

to land full weight against a pine trunk.

Only Cotton's head and shoulders showed above the rim. He had braced himself with one foot against a scraggly juniper, and he was firing slowly and coolly. Before they could pull up, Cotton had lanced a bullet into another man's middle that took him out of the saddle in a rolling fall. It had taken only seconds for Cotton's two shots, but those seconds were enough to send the five remaining men out of saddles and scrambling for cover. Cotton put two bullets into the log that sheltered the man who had been with Runt. Then there was a strange silence while the smoke and dust gradually drifted down the mountain.

One hour passed. Then two. Once Deuce Hinson showed his head, and almost got it blown off, Cotton's bullet missing by an inch. The sun was almost behind the peaks of the Cascades now. It had been in Cotton's mind to slip down from the rim, leading his black, and ride toward the river. There was no moon, and by following the creek, there would be little chance that he could be tracked. Then his plan was changed by Harriman, who leaped from behind the deadfall pine log for the rim. Cotton shot at him twice, and missed.

Below Cotton the canyon made a twist. From where he stood he could not see what Harriman was doing. He dared not take his eyes from the four men he had cornered; yet he had to know what Harriman was doing. There was no answer to it. They had him boxed. He could not go downstream if Harriman was in the bottom of the canyon. His one possibility was to get to the opposite rim of the canyon, and there was small chance of his succeeding in that if Harriman was below him.

"Drennan." It was Abernethy's voice.

"O.K.," Cotton called. "Come on into the open and we'll talk it over with hot lead."

Harriman's presence around the point of the canyon below Cotton worried him. He tried to watch the four men on top, and watch for Harriman, and couldn't do both.

140 WAYNE D. OVERHOLSER

"I don't care to be filled with lead," Abernethy shouted. "If you're smart, you'll surrender. The law wants you for the killing of Jackson Malloy. Throw away your gun, and come up with your hands over your head. I'll guarantee that you'll be taken safely to Antioch to await trial."

"Go to hell," Cotton yelled, and drove a bullet into the log in front of Abernethy.

The man in front of him who had been with Runt opened up then, but the light was too thin for straight shooting. Cotton saw his head, and sent him ducking back. He levered another shell into his rifle. Then it happened. Harriman had crawled around the point, and from the screen of a small juniper, fired twice at Cotton. The first one missed. Cotton pulled his Winchester to his shoulder, but he didn't squeeze the trigger. Harriman's second bullet got him in the right thigh, and sent him sprawling down the canyon wall, his rifle flying from his hands. There was no pain at the moment. Only a dullness that might have come from a smashing club blow on the muscles of his thigh.

Above the racket of rolling rocks and sliding dirt as his body pinwheeled downward, he heard Harriman's triumphant yell, "Got him, Mitch. Fight's over with."

Chapter Fifteen
Breath of the Devil

COTTON WASN'T KNOCKED OUT. HE ROLLED TO THE CANYON floor, and turned on over into the creek. The icy water drove the faintness from him, and sent pain racking through his body. He pulled back out of the water, and stared upward. Abernethy and the others had reached the rim and were peering down, but they had lost him in the gloom of the canyon.

"Don't see nothing," Abernethy said. "Sure you got him, Keno?"

"You're damned right," Harriman said jubilantly. "Must have hit him center. He was so busy talking to you, and answering whoever shot at him that he didn't see me. I missed the first one. Light was kind o' bad, but I sure got him the next time. You see that juniper? Well, he had a foot against the trunk. Purty steep there, and I sure knocked him loose. He went rolling down there like a greased pig sliding into hell."

"Go get the carcass," Abernethy said. "We'll take it to town."

"Aw, Boss," Pinch Gould groaned. "It's a mile down there, and it'd be five back if I had to pack that galoot."

"Take your horse," Harriman said disgustedly. "That black he was riding must be down there somewhere. Fetch him back if you find him."

Silence from the rim then, and Cotton knew they had gone after the horses. He knew, too, that there was no more fight in him, that he was bleeding badly. There would be no life, either, if they found him. In his dazed brain was a notion that he heard the low rumble of falls. As he wadded his bandanna into a ball, and held it against the bullet hole, it came to him that these were the falls, and that in them was a refuge. He crawled through the shallow water and into the spray. The last thing he remembered before he fainted was working his way round the edge of the pool and on to the wet gravel beyond. There he fell face down, and lay without motion.

Full darkness came before Pinch Gould and Deuce Hinson reached the canyon floor. They cursed as they peered into the night blackness, and saw nothing.

"There's no use looking around down here, Boss," Gould yelled. "Blacker'n the inside of a bull's belly. He might be lying under my feet for all I'd know."

"O.K.," Abernethy called back. "You stay there till morning, Pinch, and bring him in. Deuce, you come back up here. Go track Ramsay and Brown and tell 'em the job's done. Have 'em light a shuck for Broken Ring."

"Hell's bells!" Gould yelled. "You ain't gonna leave me down here with a dead man, are you?"

"Dead men don't hurt nobody," Harriman roared. "It's the live ones you've gotta look out for."

Gould swore fiercely. "I'll build me a fire," he told Hinson, "so mebbe the ghost won't get me. I'd rather sit with a dozen tough live men than I would with one dead one."

"You ain't giving the orders, Pinch," Hinson chuckled. "For once I get the best of it. You can sit with the carcass while I go riding through the brush."

BUCKAROO'S CODE   143

*   *   *

When Cotton came to he could not remember for a time where he was nor what had happened. He was conscious of his aching thigh, and of his wet clothes. Then he saw the glow of a fire through the mist. A man was hunkered beside it. Still Cotton couldn't remember what had happened, nor why he was here. He realized dully that he needed a doctor, and the bearded face of little Doc Vance seemed to float through space before him. He'd send the man who was out there after the medico.

Painfully Cotton crawled along the edge of the pool, pushing himself with his one sound foot. He cleared the falls, and was working his way over the gravel when Gould heard him, and turned to look, the red glow of the fire falling fully upon Cotton's white face. For a moment Gould stood paralyzed by fright, eyes wide in terror.

Cotton raised his hand. He tried to mumble that he wanted the doctor, but the sound that came from his lips was little more than meaningless gibberish.

"Go away," Gould screamed. "Go away. It wasn't me that shot you. It was Harriman. Go haunt him."

It did not make sense to Cotton. Again he tried to talk, tried to say he was not a ghost, but Gould could not understand. He forced his paralyzed muscles to bring him to his feet, and once there, he could not have stopped himself if he had wanted to. He went down the canyon in a hard run, falling and cursing, and getting up to run again. Slowly Cotton's mind cleared, and he realized that Gould had thought he was dead. He felt a sticky warmth on his thigh, and thought dully the wound was bleeding again.

He wondered how long he had lain there, and had no idea until daylight began its slow coming to the earth. He lay, staring at the black rim until it was fully light, the grim truth finally seeping into his consciousness. It was impossible for him to get out of the canyon by himself. He might as well have died when Harriman's bullet struck him as to lie here, and die by inches.

Cotton crawled to the edge of the creek, dipped his hand into the water, and drank. Then he fainted again. There Sandra Taney found him an hour later. She had been searching since dawn, and a few minutes before she saw Cotton she had found his horse on the rim.

The next hours were a dim, distorted nightmare to Cotton. Somehow Sandra got him into his saddle, tied him there, and led the black downstream until she found a place where the canyon walls sloped back gently from the stream. Afterward Cotton could vaguely remember being jolted for what seemed an eternity, being partly carried and partly dragged into the cabin, and put to bed in Sandra's lean-to. He seemed unable to help her, and yet he was conscious enough to wonder how so slim and small a girl could have the strength that was Sandra Taney's.

Cotton fainted again. Later the fever came. Sandra looked at the wound, and shook her head. She had dressed it, but it needed more than she could do. Cotton turned and twisted and called for June. In Sandra jealousy burned its hot path.

"I love you," she whispered. "I saved your life, but it's June that you want." She thought of her sister marrying Jackson Malloy, and what she had told Cotton. She said aloud, "You can't fight a woman's love for a man, no matter how rotten that man might be. That's what I said, Cotton, and here I am, loving a man who isn't rotten like Malloy was, but who doesn't even know I exist." Her lips came together then, forming a thin, red line. "I'll get the sawbones, Cotton, but I'm afraid June can't come."

Sandra made him as comfortable as she could. For a moment she stood looking down at him, thinking how thin his face was and how white, how his great strength had gone from him, leaving him entirely helpless and in her keeping. The wolf pack had brought him to this, and did not know it. Pain stabbed her when she thought that if any of them were around, and found him, he would be unable to protect himself. For a moment she considered staying, and instantly knew she

BUCKAROO'S CODE   145

had to go. He would die unless he had the doctor. On the other hand, Harriman probably thought Cotton was already dead. The chances were good she could get back with the medico before they started the hunt again-if they did.

Sandra went out, closing the door behind her. She saddled her horse, and rode north, circling Broken Ring and riding cautiously, stopping often to listen. There was little she could say if she were stopped, no excuse she could give for her trip to town that would be believed if they were suspicious.

Doc Vance had another idea about returning after he had listened grimly to what Sandra told him. He said, "We're lucky he's still alive. I'll hike out right now. You get a room in the hotel, and get yourself some sleep. I'll ride his horse out, and swap him for my black."

"But you might need . . ." Sandra began.

"Yeah," Vance said quickly. "I might need a pile of things which I won't get. Suppose some of Harriman's hellions catch up with me? If I'm alone I can think up a yarn that will do. If I've got you along, it'll look plumb bad. You stay here. I'm riding alone."

Slowly Sandra nodded. She said, "All right. I'll be out tomorrow."

"I'll stay there till you come," the medico said.

Vance waited several minutes after Sandra had gone. Then he locked his office, and went back to his barn. He had been keeping Redman since he had given his black to Cotton. He was saddling the big roan when Deuce Hinson came in.

"Howdy, Deuce," Vance said affably. "Haven't seen you for quite a spell."

"Not since you took Cotton out o' here in a pine box," Hinson exploded. "Dang your ornery hide, Doc. You sure made a fool out o' me."

"It wasn't me that did it," Vance said, leading Redman out of the stall.

"Abernethy about killed me for letting you . . ." Hinson

scowled. "Hey, what you mean, it wasn't you that made a fool out o' me?"

"Just what I said, Deuce. It isn't me that's making a fool out of you. It's mostly nature, but in your case, you're making a fool out of yourself by keeping on with Abernethy and Harriman. It's like I said. Keep it up, and purty soon you'll wind up in hell along with Toad Maxon."

"Yeah, I remember that there sermon you preached," Hinson growled. "What I want to know is what you're doing with Cotton's roan. Didn't you know Cotton was dead?"

"No, I didn't. When did it happen?"

"Oh, a couple of days ago. Mebbe more. I just don't recollect. We'd been combing the Wishbones for him, and finally jumped him. He was holed up just below the rim, and he was playing hell till Keno got him. We didn't find the body, but I reckon it's there all right. Funny thing happened. Abernethy put Pinch Gould to watching. It was plumb dark, and we couldn't find the body. That night Pinch swears Cotton's ghost came out and ha'nted him. Pinch is sick in bed. Reckon he was mighty nigh scared to death." Hinson snorted a laugh. Then he sobered, and eyed the medico suspiciously. "I'm asking you what you're doing with that there roan?"

"It's Cotton's bronc," Vance answered patiently as he swung into the saddle. "I gave him my black. We just sort of made a swap. Well, so long, Deuce. See you later."

"Yeah, but . . . Hey, wait a minute. Where you going, Doc?"

"Down to Slow Spring, Deuce. Sandra Taney rode in today. Said she had a man down there that needed a doc. Must be Santiam Jones or Bill Curry. Guess they're the only ones working for her, aren't they?"

"I reckon, but we need you at Broken Ring, Doc. Pinch is plumb sick, and we got another man with a bullet nick on him that Cotton put there the other night."

"O.K.," Vance said. "I'll stop on my way north. I've got to go to Slow Spring first. This hombre was hurt purty bad,

BUCKAROO'S CODE

the way the girl tells it. See you later, Deuce," and Doc Vance left the alley in a cloud of dust.

The medico stayed in Sandra's cabin until Cotton's fever broke.

"You're O.K., son," Vance said briskly. "You lost a hell of a lot of blood, and that bullet hole looked pretty bad, but if you'll behave yourself, you'll be fit as a fiddle before you know it. This fight hasn't begun yet. It's sure up to you to get back into it."

"I feel like a fool," Cotton whispered. "I don't reckon I ever was laid up like this before. Making Sandra wait on me hand and foot."

"I don't mind," Sandra said quickly.

"I'd like to see June," Cotton said. "I reckon she ain't interested in me no more, but I'd sure like to see her."

"You called for her," Sandra told him, "when I first had you here, so when I was in town I talked to her. She said she was still busy taking care of her father."

"June said . . ." Doc Vance began, whirling on Sandra. Then he checked himself. "Don't you worry none, Cotton. I reckon June will be out here one of these days."

Cotton closed his eyes. "A lot to be done," he murmured, "and time's running purty short."

"You've got lots of time, son," Vance said. "Abernethy isn't in any hurry to show what he's up to."

"What did they do to you after you got me out of town the other day?" Cotton asked.

"Not a blasted thing," Vance answered. "Abernethy was sure mad. So was Harriman. But Alcott didn't hold it against me. Reckon he was glad you got away. The whole thing went against his grain. I've done some talking and quizzing around. A lot of folks are beginning to wonder what Abernethy is up to, and what's behind some of this monkey business. Don't set well for that pack of gunslingers to hang around. Wasn't so bad when Malloy and Donahue was alive, but it doesn't make

148   WAYNE D. OVERHOLSER

sense for a man who claims to be a millionaire to hang on to that gun pack."

"Maybe he'll let them go now that he thinks Cotton is dead," Sandra said.

"No." Vance shook his head. "He's got too many irons in the fire that we can't see. He's sure got something that isn't on the level." He eyed Cotton a moment. "Son, I'll give you one idea to kick around in your head while you're lying here. Slim Brown drove the stage in the day Abernethy hit Antioch. Remember?"

"Yes. I remember."

"The funny thing is Brown hadn't been driving very long. Nobody much seems to know where he came from or anything about him."

"That isn't so queer," Cotton said. "A lot of fiddle-footed gents drift through here."

"Yeah, but here's the funny part. Brown didn't make another run. He drew his time, and he's been riding with Harriman's bunch since then."

Cotton rubbed a hand over his stubbly face. "I'm not very strong in the head right now, Doc. What sense does it make?"

"Maybe none," Vance answered. "Maybe quite a bit. With Brown handling the ribbons, and with only one passenger, how do we know what happened on the way south? Soon as you get on your feet, Cotton, I think you'd better ride north. If we knew just who got on that stage, how much dinero there was, and maybe something about Slim Brown, we'd be able to work the kinks out of the twine."

"I'll do it," Cotton said.

"O.K. I'll be moving along. Take care of him, Sandra."

"All right," Cotton said, and watched the medico go out with Sandra.

After Vance had saddled the black, he motioned for Sandra to come to him. He said sternly, "You were lying about seeing June, weren't you?"

"Yes," Sandra whispered, looking him squarely in the eye. "A woman has to fight for what she wants."

BUCKAROO'S CODE   149

"It won't work," Vance said roughly. "You've done a lot for him. You've done more than June has. I'm not arguing that, but there's one thing I'm damned sure of. He loves June, and June is in love with him. I know that. Let them alone, and eventually they'll get together."

"I don't intend to let them alone," Sandra said grimly. "You don't get anything out of life unless you fight for it. I aim to fight for what is rightfully mine."

"All you'll get is a pile of mean memories," Vance said softly. "Suppose you do get Cotton. After while you'll see he isn't happy. You'll see his eyes light up whenever June comes around. Then you'll hate yourself. There's another man for you somewhere. Don't take June's."

"He isn't June's man until she gets him," Sandra said. "If I get him he's mine, and I'll hold him. You'll see. His eyes won't light up when June comes around. They'll light up for me. If June loves him, she's had a funny way of showing it. I don't know what their trouble was, but there's something between them."

"I don't know about that." Vance stared at the cabin thoughtfully. "I reckon it wasn't any more than a chunk of foolish pride." He pinned his gaze on Sandra's doll-like face. "You're pretty as sin, and you know it. I'm not saying you won't get Cotton. I've got a hunch you will if you're crooked enough, and lie to him enough, but I'm telling you one thing. No woman ever got anywhere throwing herself at a man like Cotton. He'll do his own choosing."

Then Doc Vance stepped into the saddle, and rode away. For a long time Sandra stood watching him. Then she said firmly, "I will fight for what I want." She wheeled into the cabin, and went directly to the lean-to. When she saw Cotton was sleeping, she closed the door, and went outside again.

That evening when she brought Cotton his supper, she said, "You didn't really want June, did you, Cotton? I can do anything for you she can."

Cotton grinned. "I reckon you can, Sandra. I'm sure grateful,

WAYNE D. OVERHOLSER

and I reckon I'll never be able to repay you."

"I don't want to be repaid," Sandra said. She thought of telling him what she did want, and changed her mind. That was one thing Doc Vance had been right about. She would never get anywhere throwing herself at Cotton. "I'm sure sorry June wouldn't come."

"I guess I didn't expect it," Cotton said. "Just kind o' hoped."

Later, when Cotton had finished eating, Sandra took his plate into the other room. A moment later she ran back into the lean-to, fear showing itself upon her face in a way Cotton had never seen it. She said breathlessly, "Abernethy and Harriman are coming up the mountain."

Chapter Sixteen

Hideout

IT TOOK A MOMENT FOR THE FULL SIGNIFICANCE OF WHAT Sandra had said to sink into Cotton's consciousness. Then he motioned toward the gun belt that lay in the corner. "Hand it to me. Then stay out of the way."

Sandra pulled the gun from holster, and gave it and the belt to Cotton. He tried to raise himself into a sitting position, and immediately fell back, his face draining of the little color that was in it.

"You can't do it," Sandra whispered. "There must be some other way."

"Doc was stopping at Broken Ring. Abernethy isn't one to miss a bet. He'll want to see who's sick here."

"I'll keep him out," Sandra said grimly as she began rummaging in her suitcase. A moment later she turned toward the bed, an armful of feminine garments in her hands. "Get down under the covers. You're going to stay there while I do a piece of play-acting. Don't even wiggle."

152   WAYNE D. OVERHOLSER

Cotton grinned weakly. "Mebbe I'll go to sleep and snore."

"Don't do it. This is a case of living through the first act, or you don't play the second."

"Mebbe I'll itch." Cotton winked at her as he slid to the wall.

"Then don't scratch."

Sandra drew the blanket over Cotton's face, then piled all the coats, hats, and skirts that she owned over him. She stepped back, studying the heap until she was satisfied that Abernethy, looking at the bed from the doorway, would not know it held anyone. Then she scattered a handful of undergarments over the rest, and stepped from the room just as Abernethy and Harriman were dismounting in front of the cabin. She closed the door behind her, and walked with pretended casualness to the front door.

Abernethy removed his Stetson. "Evening, ma'am," he said in his customary, precise way. "I don't know that I've had the pleasure of really meeting you before. My name is J. Francis Abernethy. I'm the new owner of Broken Ring."

Sandra acknowledged his greeting with a nod, and said nothing.

Abernethy neither spoke nor moved for a full minute, his blue eyes studying Sandra. She was wearing the same riding skirt and tan jacket she had worn the day Cotton had first come to Slow Spring, her yellow-gold hair bright with the evening sun upon it. She made a trim, attractive figure as she stood there, her eyes meeting Abernethy's and showing neither fear of him nor any great respect.

Abernethy must have felt the girl's unspoken antagonism, but he gave no sign of it. He said courteously, "You may have heard of Jackson Malloy's tragic death. No doubt you also have heard of this man Cotton Drennan who did the killing. At the time he got away from us. Fortunately I had completed the purchase of the ranch before Malloy was killed. I believe this area down here is considered part of my range."

Sandra drew her shoulders back. "Mr. Abernethy, if you are

BUCKAROO'S CODE
153

trying to tell me that I'll have to get off, you can save your breath."

"There is no reason," Abernethy said gently, "why we should not get along. Let's go in and talk it over."

"I'm sorry," Sandra murmured. "I should have asked you in."

There was a smug grin on Keno Harriman's thin-lipped mouth as he moved past Sandra, but Abernethy's high-boned face was quite expressionless. When he was seated, he said, "Let us take the situation as we find it, Miss Taney. Malloy is dead. Broken Ring is mine. With me money makes little difference. Primarily I am interested in good hunting and fishing. However, you must not forget that Broken Ring is *the* big outfit here. Folks live on my range because I permit them to."

"And those folks will pay a price?"

Satisfaction showed itself momentarily on Abernethy's face, and passed as his habitual cold, self-sufficient expression returned. He said, "That's right."

"If you think," Sandra blazed, "that I'll pay the price a man like you thinks a single girl will pay, you're dead wrong. I'm not interested in the favors a rich man can pay. Go see June Flagg. Perhaps she would be interested."

For once Abernethy's cool self-possession was shattered. He looked at Sandra as if he were utterly astounded. He said quickly, "You misunderstand me, Miss Taney."

"I think not," Sandra snapped. "I know what men with money think they can buy. Let me tell you one thing, Mr. Abernethy. I'm here to make my home. It isn't much now," she made an inclusive gesture at the meagerly furnished cabin, "but it will be. You can shove some folks, and you can kill others, but you'll have to give a woman consideration that you wouldn't give a man. If you doubt that, go ahead and have me killed like Luke Bray and his wife were killed."

"I know nothing about that," Abernethy said. "I came here to make a deal. I can make you trouble, or we can get along. The choice is yours. If we are to get along, you'll cooperate with me. And don't count too much on being a woman. If you are going to make a man's living in a man's land, you'll play by men's rules."

"Hell, Mitch," Harriman exploded, "were wasting time. Let's get the job done."

Abernethy whirled on him. He said savagely, "Shut up, you lame-brained fool, or get out."

Anger blazed across Harriman's hard, thin face. His flinty eyes locked momentarily with Abernethy's. Slowly he regained control of himself. He said hoarsely, "O.K., Boss. Play your string out."

Abernethy turned back to Sandra, his expression coldly placid. "I'm sorry, Miss Taney, but in a country like this sometimes things are done without my orders. After they are done, there is nothing I can do."

"I see," Sandra whispered.

"Now to get back to our business. I mentioned that a cowboy named Drennan killed Jackson Malloy. We ran him down the other day some distance north of here. He was shot, but he may not have died. He may have been only wounded, and someone, perhaps you, has taken care of him. Doc Vance was here. Now," Abernethy's voice became suddenly grim, "where is he?"

Sandra stood up, her face showing the contempt that was in her. "It takes a lot of what we like to call courage to hunt down and kill a wounded man, doesn't it, Mr. Abernethy? You and your hired gunman can ride now. You've overstayed your welcome."

Abernethy was on his feet, face dark and cruel. His icy tone was utterly without mercy when he said, "There will be no more delay. We have come after Drennan."

Sandra's voice was mocking as she waved her hand around the room. "Why, my high-handed neighbor, you can look for yourself. Maybe I have him under the stove. Or under the bench you were sitting on. Or perhaps under those pine boughs in the corner."

BUCKAROO'S CODE 155

Harriman jerked his head at the lean-to's door. "Back there, Boss."

Abernethy nodded thoughtfully. He asked, "Who's been sleeping on those pine boughs?"

"I have," Sandra answered quite casually. "Santiam was hurt, and he was on my bed in the lean-to."

"Who's this Santiam hombre?" Abernethy asked Harriman.

"He's a long drink of water that used to buckaroo for Malloy. She got him and a fat jigger named Bill Curry to draw their time, and work for her."

"He's gone now?" Abernethy asked Sandra.

The girl nodded.

"We'll have a look," Abernethy snarled, moving toward the lean-to door.

"Wait," Sandra said angrily, stepping in front of Abernethy. "Is there any decency left in you, Mr. Abernethy? Will you give a woman any privacy at all? This is the first time I've had a chance to fix my clothes. I have them strung all over my bed. Do you have to go nosing in there?"

"Shut up," Abernethy said, pushing Sandra aside.

Harriman grinned. "That bluff won't work, gal."

As Abernethy opened the door Sandra began to cry. "I never have bothered you," she sobbed. "I don't go into your house, and paw around over your clothes. Now will you get out?"

Abernethy stood in the doorway, staring at the heaped up garments on the bed, Harriman gawking over his shoulder. "Holy jumping bullfrogs, Mitch, she was telling the truth. Nothing but . . ."

"Shut up," Abernethy snarled, slamming the door. "All right. Turn off the tears. What are you doing with Drennan's roan horse?"

"I heard the shooting," Sandra said between sobs. "It must have been the time you caught Drennan beside the canyon. I hunted for him, but didn't find any trace of him except the black he'd been riding. I brought him home. When Doc Vance was here, he said the black was his, so he took him, and left the roan."

Abernethy stood thinking about that, seeing the logic of it. He snapped at Harriman, "Go outside and take a look." He stared up at the ceiling as if thinking of an attic, and realizing there was none.

A moment later Harriman came back. "No trace of anything, Mitch."

"Reckon we figured it wrong," Abernethy said reluctantly. He reached down, cupped a palm under Sandra's chin, and tilted her face. There were real tears on her cheeks. That seemed to convince him. "You're a fool to live here by yourself. There could be something on Broken Ring for you if you could see it that way."

"If I didn't make myself clear a while ago," Sandra blazed, "perhaps this will." She swung an open palm against the side of his face, the crack of the blow ringing across the room. "Now will you get out?"

Abernethy's cheek was red where she had hit him. He stood towering over her, a grim, big-shouldered man who had spent his life taking the things he wanted, but lacking the evil needed to take the thing he wanted now. He said, "If you're smart, time will change your mind." He swung on his heel, and went out, Harriman behind him. A moment later they had mounted, and disappeared in the dusk.

Sandra stood watching them until they were gone. Then she went into the lean-to, threw her clothes from the bed, and pulled the blanket from Cotton's face. He grinned at her. "I heard most of what went on. I was kind o' boogery there for a minute."

"So was I," Sandra whispered. Suddenly she began to cry.

"I don't reckon them huckleberries will be back," Cotton said in a puzzled voice. "You sounded real convincing to me. Don't see no reason for you to cry now."

"I . . . I guess I'm crying because I feel so good," Sandra sobbed.

BUCKAROO'S CODE   157

"I reckon I'm the one who oughta be feeling good," Cotton said. "I'm thinking you're making the wrong bet when you said Abernethy would have to give a woman consideration that he wouldn't give a man. That might o' worked with Malloy, but I'm thinking Abernethy meant what he said. If you're taking cards in a man's game, you're gonna have to take hot lead same as a man. Reckon I'd better sashay into the brush before he finds me here."

"No," Sandra said sharply. She wiped the tears from her face. "I would rather die here with you than to know you had died in the woods because there was no one to look after you."

"There's only one way, I reckon." Cotton rubbed his stubbly cheek thoughtfully. "That's to fight it out till Abernethy's dead. When will Santiam and Bill be back?"

"Perhaps two weeks. Or less."

"Al Rhyman's still in town. There's Doc. Mebbe Fred Flagg if he's able to get around. That makes six."

"What are you talking about?"

"Counting the guns we've got. I'm thinking Doc's wrong. We've got to sail in and do the job right."

"Meanwhile you've got to get well." Sandra patted Cotton on the cheek. "See you in the morning."

Cotton heard her bar the front door. Full darkness came, and moonlight fell through the lean-to window and across Cotton's bed. He was thinking that he had judged Sandra wrong, that she had done everything for him a woman could do. When he was on his feet, and the fight was over, he would have to do whatever she asked. If she needed a ramrod, he'd take the job. Then, and it startled him when he realized it, he was thinking of June Flagg, and wishing he could see her.

Chapter Seventeen

Millionaire's Ghost

A WEEK AFTER ABERNETHY'S AND HARRIMAN'S VISIT COTTON limped into the main room of the cabin, using a crooked pine limb for a crutch. Later he was able to get outside, and chop a few limbs into stove wood. He was surprised and disgusted when he found himself growing tired within a few minutes. He wiped the sweat from his forehead, felt of his beard-covered face, and wished he could get back to Antioch for a shave and haircut. As he straightened up, and started back to the cabin, he saw a horse coming from the direction of Cold Creek. He took three wobbly steps toward the cabin, thinking it was one of Harriman's men, and wondering if he could get there in time to lay his hands on his gun. Then he stopped, and excitement ran wildly through him. The rider was June Flagg.

Cotton called, "Sandra. We've got company."

Sandra came to the doorway, carrying Cotton's gun belt. "Who is it?"

"You won't need that," Cotton said, grinning broadly. "It's June Flagg."

BUCKAROO'S CODE   159

"Oh." Sandra said it in surprise, as if she couldn't quite believe it. When she saw June, she said, "Oh," again, and asked, "What does she want?"

"Mebbe she brought some news, and mebbe some shells," Cotton said.

June rode up to them, smiling at Cotton, and he felt his breath come a little faster, as it always did when he saw her again. He thought briefly of that day in Antioch when he had seen her come out of the Mercantile. Despite all that had happened, she looked just as she had then: dark blue eyes bright and friendly, round-bodied, and lovely as she always was. Nor did she seem distant as if withdrawing herself from him the way she had when he had talked to her in the hotel.

"Doc tells me you've been taking quite a vacation," June said.

Cotton grinned. "Mebbe you could call it that. June, I reckon you've never really met Sandra Taney, have you? Sandra, this is June Flagg."

"Step down, June," Sandra said softly, "and come in."

"Thank you," June murmured, and dismounted.

Later, when they were in the cabin, Cotton sat stiffly on a bench while Sandra worked over the stove, ill at ease with June. This was the first time Cotton had seen them together, and he was astonished at the differences he saw in them. June was larger than Sandra, and she seemed much younger, although he thought there was little actual difference in age. That was something he could not quite understand. He had not thought of it before, but he sensed a depth of experience about Sandra that was not in June.

June went back to her mount, and returned with a small package for Cotton. "Doc sent this out," she said. "He claimed you were beginning to look like Rip Van Winkle with those whiskers, so he sent a razor to you."

"Was there any mail?" Sandra asked.

"No," June answered. "I asked before I left."

Cotton wondered why she had come, but he did not ask, nor

did he ask why she had not come when he had been flat on his back.

"How's Fred?" Cotton asked.

"He's ready to move back to the FF and start building a cabin," June answered, "but Doc won't let him. He says we'd just get ourselves killed. He wants to wait until you're well again, and he says we'll have enough on Abernethy to fix him."

Cotton told her of Abernethy's visit. He added, "I don't think Abernethy's going to make any mistakes. Either we'll move in, and smoke it out, law or no law, or else we'll find out who he really is. Then mebbe we'll have the law on our side."

"Or," Sandra added darkly, "we'll wait too long, and let Abernethy get rid of us one by one."

"But Cotton won't be ready to ride for weeks," June objected.

"Aren't there other men in this country to do the hard jobs besides Cotton?" Sandra demanded. "It seems to me he's been fighting a one-man war since this started."

"If he hadn't," June answered, "there wouldn't have been any war. It would all be in Abernethy's hands."

"Then let us leave it to Abernethy," Sandra said quickly. "There have been enough lives lost."

Cotton looked at her in surprise. "I reckon we couldn't do that. When a fight has gone this far, it's got to be wound up. Kind o' like getting into quicksand. When you get bogged up to your neck, it's plumb hard to get out of."

Sandra turned her back to Cotton, and forked bacon from the frying pan into a plate. June stared at her, a puzzled expression on her face, and silence ran out between them into a strained vacuum of sound. It was not until after they had started to eat that it was broken when Cotton said, "Funny how a man's hindsight is a darned sight better than his foresight. We was all balled up in our thinking until Malloy was beefed, and I got Donahue. Then it began to shape up, and we saw what

BUCKAROO'S CODE

caliber of a man Abernethy was, but we still don't know all that was behind it. I don't reckon we will till we dab a loop on Abernethy or Harriman, and make one of 'em talk."

Sandra shook her head somberly. "They'll die, or you'll die." She stared across the table at Cotton, and said desperately, "Get out of it. You have no stake in this fight."

"That's funny," Cotton murmured, "coming from you."

"Why is it funny?" Sandra demanded.

"It's funny because you can't do what you're trying to do as long as Abernethy is out to make himself the big mogul of this range."

"Perhaps," Sandra said. She got up, and poured a second cup of coffee for Cotton. "Abernethy dies. You die. Perhaps June or I will die. Only one thing I want to know. Why?"

"I guess," Cotton said thoughtfully, "nobody likes to cash in his chips. I've thought about it a lot since I got plugged. Never really got so close to hearing the devil chopping up his pine limbs and stoking up his furnace before. Take Luke Bray and his wife. I know they didn't want to die. They was chuck full of dreams, but them dreams died with 'em. Mebbe that's the answer, Sandra. Some folks have to die so other folks' dreams can be made more'n just dreams." He grinned at June. "I reckon it won't be weeks before I'm ready to ride. It'll come purty fast now."

"What are you getting at?" June demanded.

"I'm trying to say that Doc is plumb wrong," Cotton said bluntly. "I want you to go back to town and tell him that. Tell him and Fred and Al Rhyman and anybody else who ain't afraid to burn powder to ride out here in about five, six days. We'll go to Broken Ring, and we'll get a rope on Abernethy's neck. He'll talk, or we'll stretch it."

"You want me to tell Doc that?" June asked.

"That I do. Tell him to show up here with every man he can get within a week, or by hokey, I'll do the job myself. I let 'em chase me off Broken Ring, and they chased me out o' town. They chased me all over the Wishbones. I got myself plugged, and damned near got finished right here in this cabin. I would have if Sandra hadn't done a good job of play-acting. Now I'm done running. Soon as I can ride I'm going after 'em. "I'm . . ."

Outside a man yelled, "Hello the house."

Cotton grabbed his gun from where the belt hung behind him on the wall, jerked it from leather, and hobbled to the window. Then breath went out of him in a long and gusty sigh. He said, "Sandra, your crew's showed up, and looks like they took on another man."

Sandra ran to the door, and threw it open. Outside in the thin light of the setting fall sun, Santiam Jones and Bill Curry sat their saddles, eyes warily on the door, guns in their hands. A small, long-nosed man sat a third horse, upon his whiskery face the worried, sober look of a man who has suddenly been transplanted into a new, wild life, and is badly frightened by it.

Santiam's gaunt face broke into one of his seldom seen grins as he holstered his gun. "We was a little cagy, not knowing what had happened since we left." He looked at Cotton, and shook his head. "Who is that there tough looking varmint you got here, Miss Sandra? Is he man or brute?"

Cotton let out a howl. "Get down off that cayuse, Santiam, and I'll bust every bone in your body. Mebbe I ain't handsome like you are . . ."

"Handsome?" Bill Curry cut in, his fat face showing his indignation at the thought. "Don't even give room in your head for such a notion, Cotton. That there pulled-out length of clothesline is so danged ugly that when he saw a dog in Lakeview, I mean when the pup saw him, he laid down and died right then and there. Santiam's even skinnier'n he used to be. When we got a hotel room in Lakeview the door was locked, but he was so confounded lazy he wouldn't walk down and get the key. He just went in through the keyhole."

"There was sure a reason for that," Santiam said placidly. "That hunk o' fat couldn't get in. He had to sleep in the hall. Why, one time I slept with him, and he rolled on me. Well

BUCKAROO'S CODE 163

sir, come morning, I couldn't even find myself."

"And you've been looking for yourself ever since, haven't you, Santiam?" June asked.

"Yeah, that's right," Santiam admitted. He looked closely at Cotton. "I reckon that is Cotton behind that there brush, but he don't look right. Got kind of a wild look on his mug." Santiam dismounted. "Git down, Abby. Bill, go put these broncs away. I've got a hind quarter of venison here, Miss Sandra. I didn't know you had this here world-famous hunter with you, or I wouldn't have bothered bringing it in."

"We can use it, Santiam," Sandra said soberly, not at all amused by the talk between Santiam and Bill Curry. "Cotton has been laid up, so we haven't had any fresh meat recently."

"Laid up?" Santiam pinned his gaze on Cotton. "What the hell happened, boy? I never did see so much shrubbery on your face, and you look like you ain't et good for a month."

"That's all right enough," Cotton answered. "A lot's happened since you pulled out. I've been spending most of my time dodging Abernethy and them hired gun dogs of his."

"Whose gun dogs?" Santiam demanded. "I thought it was Donahue you was gonna bust. You was gonna 'rod Broken Ring for Malloy. Don't make sense."

"It makes plenty of sense," Cotton answered. "Donahue's dead. So's Malloy. They claim I beefed Malloy, which I didn't. Abernethy's giving the orders to Harriman, and he claims he bought Broken Ring. Leastwise he's running it."

"That reminds me," Santiam said, motioning toward the small, long-nosed man who had dismounted and stood beside him. "Seems to be some mix-up on who's who. This here gent is J. Francis Abernethy. He's the one and only, and that there square-headed hombre who got off the stage and claimed he was Abernethy was somebody else. Now don't ask me who. I just know he ain't Abernethy 'cause that's who this feller is, and they don't look alike, now do they?"

Chapter Eighteen
The Dead Returned

THEY STARED AT THE LONG-NOSED MAN IN BLANK AMAZE-
ment: Sandra, June, and Cotton. For a long time they had
suspected that the man who passed as Abernethy was not
Abernethy, but that there was a real J. Francis Abernethy still
alive and somewhere in Oregon was more than they could
accept. Slowly Cotton shook his head. "You allus had a big
name for lying, Santiam. Reckon it just comes natural to you
like telling the truth does to most folks, but this . . ."

"Now you look here, you tow-headed, bow-legged, ugly-
faced baboon," Santiam howled. "I ain't lying. I don't lie like
Bill Curry there for instance. You tell him, Abby. Mebbe he
won't call you a liar."

A brief smile touched the little man's lips. "I guess I don't
look like a brother of the famous Pierce Abernethy, do I?
Nevertheless, that's who I am. Unfortunately, I have no proof
upon me, nor do I see how I can prove it until I get a letter
describing me. I mailed one when we were in Lakeview.
The answer should be in Antioch soon. Or perhaps I could

BUCKAROO'S CODE   165

go to the Columbia, and wire for a description." He spread his hands helplessly. "Or perhaps neither would work. You see, all my money was stolen. If these men had not found me," he motioned toward Santiam and Bill, "I would not be alive."

"I think," Sandra said weakly, "we'd better go inside and sit down before we fall down."

Later, when they were seated around the table with the lamplight falling upon the little man's face, Cotton had a better chance to study him. He was about forty, Cotton guessed, and as he talked, some of the worry dropped from him as if he realized that at last he had reached shelter, and was among friends. At first glance Cotton had thought him a totally futile little man, but now he changed his mind. Abernethy's eyes were black and sharp, his chin square, and he had a way of looking directly at a man as if seeing more than was on the surface. In a different setting and with clean clothes instead of the sweat-stained, alkali-coated suit he wore, this little man would be anything but futile.

"It isn't a long story," Abernethy said, "but it comes close to being a tragic one. I have no idea what really happened. I had been corresponding with Jackson Malloy for some time about a ranch. I knew him by reputation, having heard about him from some friends who knew of ranches he had developed in Arizona. I understood he was a shrewd bargainer, but that he was square, and that he understood ranch values. He was asking one hundred thousand dollars for Broken Ring. I considered the figure too high, but I promised to come to Antioch and see it."

"Malloy had no idea what you looked like?" Cotton asked.

"None," Abernethy admitted. "Perhaps that was my error, but I did not know what was ahead. In fact, Malloy assured me this was a very peaceful country, and not at all like Arizona."

"It was peaceful enough before Malloy showed up," June said.

Abernethy gestured wearily. "Of course I knew nothing about that. I knew Malloy had gone by a different name in Arizona, and that he had been in trouble. I didn't go into that. I did establish the fact that he was the man I had heard about, and his letters sounded as if he had the sort of thing I wanted, so I sent word telling him exactly when I would reach Antioch, and he promised to meet me. I told him that I would bring twenty thousand dollars with me, and would pay the balance within the year if I bought the place. That seemed to satisfy him."

Cotton nodded somberly. "It begins to make sense. Donahue would have known about that."

"At any rate," Abernethy went on, "the stage was stopped some miles north of Antioch. There were no guns drawn at the time. A square-shouldered, well-dressed man was standing at the edge of the road. Two others were on horses, and they had an extra horse with them. When the stage stopped, the well-dressed man opened the door and told me to get out. I refused. Then one of the mounted men drew a gun and cocked it. I had no choice but to obey. They took my money and the papers I had on me. The well-dressed man got into the stage, and was studying my papers when it drove away."

"It's strange they didn't kill you then," Sandra said.

"I gathered from their talk," Abernethy said, "that they didn't want to kill me because somebody might come along. Apparently the country east of there was pretty well settled. They made a sweep into the desert, and after we were a great distance south of Antioch they made me get off the horse. The one called Pinch drew his gun to shoot me. The other one said the sound of a gunshot would be heard for miles across the desert. They argued quite a while about how they were going to kill me. Pinch said it didn't make any difference, but the other one said they weren't supposed to leave a gunshot wound in me. Finally he hit me over the head with his gun barrel. When I came to I was flat on my face in the sand."

BUCKAROO'S CODE   167

"When we found him he was walking around in circles," Santiam said, "crazy as a loon. It was three days before he could remember everything."

"Now," Abernethy said briskly, "I want to be taken to Antioch."

"June, take him to Doc," Cotton said. "He's been wanting to get the law on our side. This should do it."

"And now," Sandra said, "that we've heard this, perhaps you'll explain where my cattle are."

"Well, ma'am," Santiam said sheepishly, "as your foreman I made a decision."

"Just think of him making a decision," Bill Curry jeered, "with his brain."

"Leastwise it ain't all fat," Santiam said darkly. "Now you shut up, or I'll make lard out of what's left of you."

"What you mean, Santiam?" Cotton asked. "Looks to me like there's plenty left of him."

"Plenty, all right," Santiam admitted, "but not as much as there was. He ate too much in Lakeview, and couldn't pay for it. Well sir, the cook just put him in a frying pan, and let him simmer for a spell. When he got done, he had fifteen pounds of lard, twelve pounds of taller, and five pounds of just plain fat. Kind o' looked like goose grease."

"My cattle?" Sandra cut in.

"Oh, yeah," Santiam said mournfully. "I was trying to tell about my decision. Well, ma'am, we got them cattle out of Nevada all right, but they was plumb puny. Yes sir, you could count every rib from number one clean up to number forty-nine. We got 'em to Lakeview, and we couldn't drive 'em no longer. They was just falling right and left. If we'd brung 'em on, you could have followed our trail plumb across the desert by the bones of them puny critters."

"So?" Sandra demanded.

"So," Santiam finished, "I made arrangements to have 'em wintered in Lakeview. Me and Bill will get 'em come spring."

"In other words," Cotton said, "you figgered there wasn't

any hay here, and that there'd be too much snow before you could haul it down from French Creek."

"Well," Santiam admitted dolefully, "stripping off all the underbrush and putting it right to the point, that's it."

"Santiam couldn't tell a story without sort of fixing it up," Cotton told Sandra, "but when you get it boiled down, I guess he done right."

"Maybe so," Sandra said reluctantly, "but I wanted my cattle here. I thought . . ." Then she looked at Abernethy, and shook her head. "I guess it doesn't make any difference. If snow gets so deep here, I suppose I'd better move into town this winter."

"What's more," Cotton said, "it would be a good idea if you pulled out now. If there's a fight, I don't want you here."

"If there's a fight, I'm staying here," Sandra said stubbornly.

Abernethy had been watching her closely. Now he said, "Women are different out here. Perhaps it's the sun, or the water they drink. At any rate they are far more beautiful than they are where I came from, and they are unquestionably braver. Why you should want to stay here if there is a fight is more than I can see."

Sandra blushed with his compliment. Her blush deepened when Santiam chuckled. He said, "Must be the company of females, ma'am. He never got off no such talk as that all the way across the desert."

The next morning June took Abernethy with her when she left for Antioch. Cotton watched them disappear into the pines. He said, "Always makes me a little uneasy when I see anybody riding out in that direction. They'll get purty danged close to Broken Ring. Mebbe you boys oughta ride with 'em."

"No," Sandra said quickly. "They stay here. We may need them. Besides, there's wood to cut."

"That's right," Cotton said, "and I don't know of anything that'll bring me out of it faster than swinging an ax for a spell."

BUCKAROO'S CODE   169

"What you gonna call that jasper who's been passing as Abernethy?" Santiam asked.

"His first name is Mitch," Cotton answered. "From what Pinch Gould said, I figger his last name is Ordway."

For a week Cotton chopped wood. His appetite grew until Santiam said, "You sure got a hollow leg. That bullet hole must o' fixed it. No ordinary man could put away so much grub."

"And I'm beginning to believe I made a mistake hiring you," Sandra said tartly. "I never saw a skinny man eat so much in my life."

"Skinny man?" Santiam said, greatly offended. "Ma'am, I want you to know I ain't skinny. I'm just sort o' slender."

"You mean cadaverous," Sandra said.

"Cad . . . cad . . . cad what?" Santiam asked.

"Never mind," Cotton cut in. "What she means is that slender isn't the word."

"And as for eating," Santiam said, "what about Bill there?"

"I give up," Sandra said. "You'll have to go get another deer."

"And they ain't worth nothing when it comes to working." Cotton winked at her.

"If it were a big spread," Sandra said softly, "and you were 'rodding the outfit, they'd work. How about it, Cotton? I still would like to have you for my foreman."

Cotton met her gaze squarely. He had known this would come again, and he could not refuse her. But beyond that? When a man owes his life to a woman as he owed his to Sandra Taney, there was little he could not do if he was asked. Now he nodded gravely. "Come spring," he said, "and if it still is what you want, then you've got a ramrod."

As the week ran out Cotton watched for Doc Vance, and the men who would come with him from Antioch. By the end of the sixth day they had not come. At sundown Cotton drove the ax into the log, and shook his fist in the direction of Antioch. "Why in hell don't they come?" he demanded. "If they aren't here by morning, I'm riding ."

Santiam said, "Easy, son. Us three against that wolf pack wouldn't make a right good fight. There's no hurry. You've been waiting for a long time. Won't hurt to wait a while longer."

The result of that waiting was plain on Cotton's face. It was not in him to wait longer. He said hoarsely, "You keep putting off a fight, Santiam, and purty soon you either get so proddy you can't fight worth a damn, or else your guts run out, and the fighting isn't in you. Tomorrow I'm riding. You boys don't need to go."

"Cotton," Santiam said sharply. "I don't take kindly to them there words."

"I'm sorry." Cotton's face softened. He thought of that day when he and Santiam and Bill had stood at the bar in the Empress Saloon with Harriman and his bunch at the other end. He thought of the things that had happened, now a long time ago, and he thought again of June Flagg and how she had not gone to the dance with him. He knew now, since her visit here a week ago, that she was as far beyond his reach as she was the day she had stood beside the Flagg buckboard, and said she was going to the dance with Malloy. When she had left six days before, she had said pointedly, "I was mistaken about Sandra. I never liked blondes, but she's different."

Cotton wheeled toward the cabin, face suddenly ugly. Santiam watched him go. "Plumb proddy," he murmured. "A fight would be the same to him as a shot of forty rod would be to a drunk." Then he lifted his eyes to the cloud-gray sky. "Winter's coming, Bill," he opined. "Got the feel of snow in the air right now."

There was snow on the ground the next morning. Two inches of it. Sandra cooked breakfast for them, and stood in the doorway as they threw saddles on their mounts. Cotton swung up, raised a hand to Sandra, and rode around the cabin, Santiam and Bill Curry behind him. Try as he would, he could not forget the concern on Sandra's face as she watched him go.

BUCKAROO'S CODE   171

"We'll cross the canyon," Cotton said, "and stay in the timber till we get close. No use . . ." He reined up, eyes on a dark blot in the snow to his left. "Is that a man lying there?"

"Looks like a man all right," Santiam said.

They reined their horses to the left, and a moment later pulled up beside the man who was lying face down in the snow. Cotton dismounted, and turned the man over. Then breath went out of him audibly. The man was Jackson Malloy.

Chapter Nineteen

Death in Ice

"WELL, I'LL BE A DOGGONED SON OF A LOW DOWN, MUT-toneating sheepherder," Santiam muttered." "Thought you said this monkey was dead."

"I sure thought he was, and he's not far from it now," Cotton said. He thought how Sandra felt toward Malloy: yet there was nothing to do but take him back to the cabin at Slow Spring. "We'll put him on your bronc, Santiam, and you can get up behind me."

"Miss Sandra don't like this galoot," Santiam said.

"There's no other place to take him," Cotton returned.

Sandra didn't say any of the things Cotton had thought she would when she saw who it was. "Put him on the bed. Is he wounded?"

"Didn't see no bullet wound," Cotton answered, "but he's mighty near frozen to death." He stood staring down at Malloy's thin white face, thinking how far down the man had gone, how different he was from the swaggering, cigar-chewing cowman who had come into the Empress that day and said J. Francis

BUCKAROO'S CODE   173

Abernethy would be on the stage. Malloy had loved himself and he had loved money. Now it looked to Cotton as if both life and money had run short for Jackson Malloy.

"He's sure skinny," Santiam said. "Mebbe that Mitch Ordway hombre ain't been feeding him much."

"We'll stay here till he goes one way or the other." Cotton stood watching Malloy, still unable to believe this was the man who, a few weeks ago, had felt himself above everybody and everything else on White River range, this man who had built Broken Ring for no better purpose than to sell it for a profit.

When Malloy's eyes did open, there was the look in them of a man who was utterly lost. Terror came into them when they fixed on Sandra's face. "I'm in hell," he whispered. "They've sent you down here to punish me."

"You're not in hell yet," Sandra said.

Malloy's dark eyes turned to Cotton, then Santiam, and finally Bill Curry. "I guess I'm still alive, and in Slow Spring cabin. That right?"

"That's it," Cotton said. "What's been happening at Broken Ring?"

"Plenty." Again Malloy's eyes came to Sandra. "You're Sandra, aren't you? You're her sister?"

Sandra nodded, unable to speak. Cotton was surprised by what he saw on her face. Sandra Taney had dreamed of revenge for so long that she had become warped by it, but now that the moment was here, she was finding no satisfaction in it. Perhaps she was feeling what Cotton had told her she would, that if she killed Malloy she would have him in her dreams, that his death would not bring her sister back.

"Get me some paper, pen and ink," Malloy said, urgency in his voice. "A man doesn't always know, but I think I've got to the jumping-off place. There's one thing I want to free my soul from before I cash in."

When Sandra left the lean-to, Malloy tried to grin at Cotton. "I had it all figured, Cotton. I didn't count on that damned Mitch Ordway being what he is. I thought he was Abernethy.

I didn't know different until you shot Donahue. Seems like Ordway used to be a lawyer for a railroad in California. He got into trouble, and ran to Arizona. That was where he hooked up with Donahue and Harriman. Donahue had his claws into me, and when we got up here, and he saw what I had in mind, he got the idea it would be a nice set-up for Ordway."

Sandra came back with the paper, pen and ink. Malloy flexed the fingers of his right hand, and shook his head. "Too stiff. Couldn't get many clothes when I pulled out of Broken Ring. They'd been starving me, and I guess Ordway thought I didn't have the strength to make a run. Anyhow, I got a horse, and headed here. I knew damned well I couldn't get to town. Then I guess I went to sleep in the saddle, and fell out."

"About Ordway?" Cotton prompted.

"Well, Donahue wrote to him what was happening up here, that I had Abernethy on the string. It was Ordway's idea to impersonate Abernethy. He's plenty smart, that hombre. Donahue was tricky, but Ordway figures things out. He came north, and hid out somewhere along French Creek until Abernethy came up on the stage. Donahue knew everything about Abernethy that I knew, so it was easy enough to fix it so they'd stop the stage north of Antioch, take Abernethy off, and have Ordway climb on. I sucked in just like they figured I would. They took the money and Abernethy's papers, and killed him."

"They thought they did," Cotton said. "Abernethy is alive, and is in Antioch right now."

"The hell," Malloy muttered. He closed his eyes wearily. "That's about the size of it, Cotton. The day you shot Donahue they had me in a back bedroom. They wanted me to sign Broken Ring over, and tell 'em where I kept my dinero. That's one thing Donahue didn't know. I wouldn't do it. They took me back to the office. Donahue shot me in the chest when you came in, but he shot high because they didn't want me to die right then. Seems like they had it figured that you'd have an empty gun, and Donahue would cut you down. Something

BUCKAROO'S CODE

went wrong, and you got Donahue. Ordway was fit to be tied after that."

Cotton smiled grimly. "I reckon he would be. They said you'd been murdered, and Ordway claimed I did it."

"I mighty near did cash in. I got over the bullet wound, but Ordway kept starving me. He's a good man with a pen, so he forged my signature to the papers, but he wanted the dinero I had put away, and I wouldn't tell him where it was. If he'd got my money after getting Abernethy's, and then stolen the herd, they'd have a big chunk of cash to split. I guess that's what he really wanted."

Malloy closed his eyes again. "I never knew what it was to be tired before. Reckon I can't write. You do it, Sandra. I'll sign it." He opened his eyes then. "You gents mosey out, will you? This is the wind-up. I know it. Might be fitting if I died here beside the sister of the girl whose death I caused."

Cotton went out, Santiam and Bill Curry behind him. Cotton closed the door. "Funny thing," he said softly, "how things wash out. He was headed here. Reckon he wanted to see Sandra, and just couldn't make it. When he ran into Ordway he met up with a man who was a sight tougher'n he was. Mebbe that's why he got to thinking about what he'd done to Sandra's sister."

"What happened to her sister?" Santiam asked.

Cotton told him. Then he said softly, "Sandra's not the girl she was that first time we saw her in Antioch. She had Malloy right where she wanted him, but it didn't feel good. You could tell that by looking at her." Suddenly Cotton stiffened, his eyes whipping to the front window. "This is it, boys, and that damned Doc ain't here."

Cotton pulled his gun from leather, and wheeled toward the door. Santiam and Bill Curry had taken their looks, and swore aloud. Coming toward the cabin was the full string of Harriman's gun hands.

"Holy jumping caterpillars," Santiam groaned. "We can't fight that army."

"We've got to," Cotton said grimly, "and we can't stay inside. This shack isn't bulletproof by a long shot, and I don't want Sandra on the receiving end."

Santiam looked at him sharply. "You're sweet on that gal, ain't you?"

"Hell, no," Cotton snapped. "She just saved my life. That's all." He held the door open a crack, watching the horsemen warily approach. "Don't see Ordway. Mebbe he's in the back. There's one hombre way down the mountain. Yeah, that's him. Harriman's in front. Ramsay's behind him. There's Pinch Gould and Deuce Hinson, and the whole damned, dirty coyote pack. They must o'tracked Malloy."

"They won't want him killed," Santiam said. "Mebbe we can make a dicker."

"The hell with any dicker," Cotton snapped. He rubbed his chin reflectively. "Santiam, you go out and palaver with 'em. You, too, Bill. Get 'em off their horses, and get 'em bunched. Then I'll stick my nose into it, and we'll see how it goes."

"Suicide," Bill Curry grunted.

"You're too fat to die," Santiam growled. He eased his gun in leather, and went out, Bill Curry behind him.

Cotton had stepped back so that he would not be seen. Then, as Curry jerked the door shut, Cotton moved back to it, held it open a fraction of an inch, and put his eye to it.

"What are you gents doing up here?" Santiam bawled.

"Don't you know this is Sandra Taney's outfit? She don't want no trespassers coming around. Now get the hell out of here."

Harriman laughed as he swung down from his horse. "Get out of the way, you washed-out hunk o' bean pole. We're looking for Malloy."

"Thought he was dead," Curry said.

"He's gonna be," Harriman snarled, his flinty eyes moving from Santiam to Curry and back to Santiam. "Now you boys can get tough, and die right here in the snow, or you can be smart, and stand aside."

BUCKAROO'S CODE   177

Ramsay was on the ground, and as he stepped around his horse, Santiam saw the cocked Colt he carried. "The boss is too damned patient," Ramsay said, "but he's finally seen the light. It's just like we did with Luke Bray. We can't afford to leave jiggers like you around when we're playing for keeps. We've got quite a stake in this game, and we're sure as hell gonna collect."

Ramsay raised his gun, and in a moment would have killed Santiam. Hinson and Gould and two other men had dismounted, and were moving toward the door of the cabin. Mitch Ordway was still sitting his horse at the back of the line, watching the play closely. Cotton wondered if Harriman or Ramsay had taken the leadership from him. Ordway was one to play it slowly and carefully. The others were not.

Ramsay's gun was lined now on Santiam's chest. "Why don't you make a play?" he sneered, "You plumb yella? I sure do hate . . ."

Then Cotton stepped into the snow, gun palmed, and the sight of him sent hands slapping gun butts, brought a howl of surprise from Keno Harriman, and with it came a chaotic merging of gun thunder, rolling smoke, screaming lead, and blood running its scarlet patterns into the snow; all one hideous maze of sight and sound.

Cotton had made up his mind before he had stepped through the door. He wanted the square-shouldered man, Mitch Ordway, who had passed as Abernethy for so long, but Ordway was taking no part in the fight. It was Harriman and Ramsay who had to die, then, and it had to be Butch Ramsay first because another second would have brought death to Santiam Jones. That was why Cotton swept his gun to big-necked Butch Ramsay and with his first shot sent him toppling into the snow like a short and heavy-trunked oak.

There were some things Cotton did not understand. A Winchester cracked from behind him, and men fell who were not under his gun. Santiam was working his .45 in the cool and regular rhythm of a man who has smelled powder smoke

178   WAYNE D. OVERHOLSER

before. Bill Curry had tried to pull his gun, but was pathetically
slow. Before it had cleared leather he had slumped forward, to
lie motionless within ten feet of Butch Ramsay's still form.

Harriman pitched a slug at Cotton, missed, and fired again.
The second bullet ripped a gash along Cotton's ribs; then he
had whipped his gun from Ramsay, and sent Harriman down
with a chunk of lead in his chest. Cotton whirled toward
the plunging mass of horses, and momentarily held his fire.
Gould was down. Deuce Hinson was on his hands and knees,
and even as Cotton turned toward him, he fell flat out, face
nose-deep in the snow.

Then Cotton understood what had happened. Jackson Malloy
had taken chips in the game. It had been his firing from the
window that had disorganized the gun crew. That, and the
sight of Keno Harriman and Butch Ramsay going down before
Cotton's gun. One more man came rolling out of his saddle.
That was enough. The rest of them reined around, and drove
the steel home.

Cotton and Santiam emptied their guns at the fleeing horsemen. Ordway was not among them. Nor was he on the ground.
Cotton had a look at Bill Curry, saw the fat man had nothing more than a bullet crease. Santiam Jones had a shoulder
wound. Jackson Malloy was dead. Sandra was standing over
him, a gun in her hands.

"Malloy deeded Broken Ring to me," she told Cotton as if
she still could not exactly believe it. "Said there was no use in
telling me about my sister. Since Dad was dead, Broken Ring
was rightfully mine."

Cotton motioned toward Malloy. "How did he get killed?"

"He heard the ruckus out here. Just as you went through the
door, he took the Winchester down from the wall. He shot
a man at the same time you got the big-necked one. He hit
another one, too. Then somebody shot him. I don't know who
it was, but the shot came from down the mountain."

"Ordway," Cotton muttered. "Funny he didn't try to get
me."

BUCKAROO'S CODE 179

"He couldn't see you," Santiam said. "From where he was that bunch of horses was between you and him. He was gone by the time the rest of 'em figgered they had enough."

"I reckon Doc will be along," Cotton said."You patch Bill and Santiam up, Sandra. Santiam, you look them polecats over. If any of 'em are still alive, take care of 'em."

"What are you . . ." Santiam began.

"I've got a piece of business to do," Cotton said, and went out to his horse. He mounted, and rode down the mountain to where Mitch Ordway had stayed. The man was a coward. Harriman and Ramsay and the rest had come in for the kill, but Ordway had carefully stayed in the back. It might mean that he was no longer running the outfit, or it might mean he wanted no part of a fight. Now, as Cotton thought over all the things that had happened these last weeks, he could not remember Ordway's doing any fighting he could avoid.

Cotton found the tracks of Ordway's horse. The routed gunmen had headed west, but Ordway's tracks led east into the Wishbones. Cotton followed them, not knowing what was in the man's evil brain, but certain that only his death could bring peace to White River range. Hour after hour Cotton held to the chase, climbing higher into the mountains. It was late afternoon when he drew up, and sat staring at the tracks, wondering what Ordway was trying to do. He had been following an eastern course. Now, with apparently no reason, he had turned directly north into a broken country dotted with lava upthrust and strewn with deadfall jack pines.

Suddenly Cotton saw he had let himself be sucked into a trap. Ordway might be anywhere in the lava. His gun might be lined on Cotton now. That would be the way a man like Mitch Ordway would fight. As dangerous as a treed panther, and more treacherous. Cotton did not move for a time, feeling the presence of the other man, and not knowing what he should do. If he rode directly into the lava, he would be cut down instantly. If he turned and rode down the mountain, he would get a slug in the back.

180   WAYNE D. OVERHOLSER

Then Cotton's mind was made up for him. In a cold, precise voice, Ordway said, "Get your hands up, Drennan. This is the end of the trail."

Cotton lifted his hands, eyes searching the lava, and seeing no one.

"Good," Ordway said. "You know you are about to die, don't you, Drennan?"

Cotton gave no answer. Still his eyes searched the lava, and still he saw no one. Ordway's chill, merciless laugh came to him. "There is no use to look for me, Drennan. I am behind a wall of rock. I have a hole through which I can see you, and through which my gun is pointing. Now I do not like to fight. Men like Keno Harriman and Butch Ramsay can always be bought to do that. Today they took the bit into their own teeth, and you see where it got them. I'm done. I was willing to ride out of this country, and never come back, but you were not willing that I should. You followed me, and you decreed your own death by so doing."

The man was scared. Cotton saw that from the unnecessary talk, yet at the moment he could see no way of making a break that would promise any kind of a chance. He said, "You're a purty smart hombre, Ordway. You figger you didn't make any mistakes, but you did."

"I made my mistake by letting you shoot Donahue," Ordway said. "That was Red's own idea. I mean about taking the powder out of the shell. He was very tricky. When I lost him, I lost the man who could keep the plug-uglies in hand. Harriman and Ramsay and men like that have no brains. Trigger-happy plug-uglies. That's all. Donahue was different. The second mistake I made was trying to let the law handle you in Antioch. I should have had you shot from ambush."

"You made another mistake, Ordway. Abernethy is alive. He was picked up by Bill Curry and Santiam Jones in the desert."

Silence then. Cotton thought Ordway was thinking that over, and that his one hope of life depended on carrying

BUCKAROO'S CODE   181

on a conversation until some sort of a chance to make a play developed. Then he saw he was wrong. Ordway came around a high lava upthrust, leading his horse, his cocked gun in his hand.

"You were wise not to try to run," Ordway said, still very precisely and very coldly. "I'm a dead shot. I daresay Jackson Malloy is dead."

"Very dead," Cotton agreed.

"I was quite a distance from the cabin this morning, but I got him. I'm only sorry you were standing in such a position that I couldn't see you, and I did not care to wait."

"You're a yellow dog," Cotton shouted. "A damned, dirty yellow dog. I can't understand why you didn't plug me just now."

"The answer is simple. A gunshot might have brought help. I have no way of knowing how many are around here. So I'll conduct you forward a few hundred feet to an ice cave that I discovered when we were playing hide-and-seek with you in these mountains. There your body will rest for ages, and it will never be found. Get off your horse, and walk straight ahead."

For a long moment Cotton's eyes locked with Abernethy's chill blue ones, and he saw the ex-lawyer meant to do exactly what he said. Cotton said, "I suppose it would not be in you to let me put my hands down and make a fair fight of it."

"A very foolish proposal," Ordway snapped. "I am not a gambler. I play only sure things. Get moving."

Cotton turned, and walked slowly ahead of Ordway. Never before had he been in a tight like this. His gun was still in his holster, but it might as well have been a thousand miles from where he stood. His arms ached from being held so long above his head. During the few minutes that it took them to reach the cave, one idea after another raced through Cotton's brain, and was promptly discarded.

When they came to the cave opening, Ordway said, "Hold it, Drennan. I thought I might let you keep your gun. You'd freeze to death just as soon if you had it as if you didn't. However, after thinking about it, I've decided I might just as well have it for a souvenir. Unbuckle your gun belt and let it drop."

Cotton had turned, and was watching Ordway's face closely. Never, Cotton thought, had he seen a man show less feeling. The fact that he was about to commit murder was affecting him not at all.

"All right," Ordway said coldly. "I said to let that gun belt go."

As Cotton's fingers fumbled with the buckle, he considered the chance of going for the gun in the face of Ordway's naked Colt, and decided against it. He said, "You're a fool for trying to cross the desert this time of year, Ordway. You don't know the trail, and you won't find water. Chances are you'll freeze if you don't starve."

"It's better than staying here," Ordway said indifferently, "and I will carry with me the satisfaction of knowing that your body will be preserved for the first man who explores this cave."

The gun belt dropped. Ordway nodded. "Very well. Now go down ahead of me. At the back of the first chamber the ice floor slopes sharply toward an opening in the back wall. That leads into a hole that must go clear to hell. We tossed rocks into it, and we never heard them strike. That's where you're going, Drennan. If there is a bottom, and you don't get killed by the fall, you'll freeze to death."

"If it goes clear to hell," Cotton said lightly, "I guess it will be plumb warm at the other end."

"It seems odd for a man to joke when he is about to die," Ordway said.

They had reached the bottom of the cave. Before them stretched the ice-floored cave. At the far end of the chamber the cave narrowed until it was eight feet or less in diameter. Beyond that would be the deep hole Ordway had mentioned, opening, probably, into a second chamber like the one they

BUCKAROO'S CODE   183

were in. Cotton looked up. The rock roof of the cave was criss-crossed by deep breaks, giving the appearance of huge boulders hanging overhead ready to fall at any second. Cotton had been in many caves in central Oregon, and he knew that the roofs were much more solid than they looked. The chances were that Ordway was not familiar with these caves, and he knew that the man was at heart a coward. In that instant an idea came to Cotton that carried promise with it.

"Well," Ordway said in his precise way, "what do you think of it?"

"A cool spot to spend eternity," Cotton answered as he moved along over the slippery ice, holding to the rock-jutting wall. "You know, Ordway, there's a heap of difference between just plain murdering a man like you're doing, and killing him in a fair fight. Now you don't see that, but how many men have you ever murdered?"

"Why, none," Ordway answered.

"Then you don't know anything about it." Cotton laughed easily. "That will be my revenge. This thing you're doing will never be out of your mind. You'll wake up screaming in fear. You'll picture me lying down there. You'll imagine how it seems and feels to freeze to death. Ordway, you'll go crazy. Completely, raving crazy."

While he had been talking Cotton had been moving carefully along the rock wall until he had reached the end where the cave narrowed and dropped into a great abyss. There was a slight indentation in the rock wall between him and the back, forming a sort of alcove. At the edge of this Cotton stopped. For a moment Ordway had said nothing. He stood, cocked gun still lined on Cotton, face shadowed by the gloom of the cave.

"Are you afraid to die, Ordway?" Cotton asked casually.

Suddenly Ordway began to tremble, whether from fear or rage Cotton couldn't tell. For the first time since Cotton had known him his mask of cool indifference broke. He burst into a volley of lurid curses as he followed Cotton on into the cave. When he stopped cursing for want of breath, Cotton jeered a laugh. "You're breaking, Ordway. All the fine scheming you've done has come down on your head. All this dinero you was gonna make by robbing folks is nothing more than a dream."

"Shut up," Ordway raged. "I've heard enough. You're gonna die with a slug in your guts, and I'll heave your body into the hole. You'll slide all the way to hell."

Chapter Twenty
A Man's Choice

IN ORDWAY THE DESIRE TO KILL WAS A FIERCE AND DRIVING power. As his trigger finger tightened, Cotton slid back into the recess in the rock wall and stood sideways so that there was little of him to make a target for Ordway. He said, "You didn't know why I was coming back in here, did you, Ordway? It was simple enough. I wanted you far enough in here so that when you shot me you'd bring the roof in on your head. If I'm gonna die, you might as well die, too."

The gun in Ordway's hand hung at his side as his eyes turned upward.

"See them boulders up there, just hanging by a thread?" Cotton said. "One of 'em is right over your noggin. It'll make mincemeat out of you the second you squeeze trigger. Won't take nothing more'n a gunshot in here to bring that whole roof down on top of us."

Ordway stood staring upward as if paralyzed. It was then Cotton made his gamble. He leaped at Ordway, trusting that the man's innate cowardice would keep him from shooting.

186   WAYNE D. OVERHOLSER

In that he was right. Ordway saw him coming. Instead of squeezing trigger, he swung the gun barrel at Cotton's head. Cotton, expecting that maneuver, fell belly flat and slid directly at Ordway. Ordway's frantic swing of the gun barrel put him into a ludicrous, half-balanced position. Cotton, hands outstretched, caught him by the ankles, and brought him down in a breath-taking fall.

Ordway bleated in terror as he went down. He hit hard, and lay for a moment unable to move. That moment gave Cotton time to gain his feet. As Ordway rose, Cotton hit him on the jaw with a long, looping blow. Ordway sprawled headlong on the ice, falling toward the opening that led into the unexplored chasm below. There was nothing on the sloping ice to slow Ordway's progress. He traveled like a rocketing bobsled, made a futile attempt to grab at a spear point of rock, and missed. He went on through the hole and disappeared, his last desperate shriek rising behind him like a banshee's wail.

Sick at stomach, Cotton carefully made his way to the wall of the cave, and retraced his steps. He could think of no more horrible way to die; yet he could not have prevented Ordway's death. As he climbed out he thought how ironical it was that Ordway had said Cotton had decreed his own death by following him. That was exactly what Ordway had done by taking him into the ice cave.

Cotton picked up his gun belt, and buckled it on. He walked back to where he had left Redman, and climbed into the saddle. As he rode down the mountain, he wondered if Luke Bray and his wife knew what had happened. It seemed so long ago when he had stood in front of Duke Bellew's barber shop waiting for Santiam Jones and Bill Curry. The bullet gash on his ribs hurt him. Sometime during his scrambling on the ice, he had injured the leg Keno Harriman had wounded. He was hungry and he was sleepy. These things he was dully aware of. His mind kept going back to that day in town and the things he had planned; the pool game, the thick steak in Big Nose Charlie's, the drink in the Empress, the dance that night with June. Those were

BUCKAROO'S CODE 187

the things he had anticipated so long. He was still thinking of that when he put his horse away at Slow Spring. The cabin was empty. He fell into bed without building a fire or getting anything to eat.

It was noon the next day before Cotton woke. The door of the lean-to was open. The pungent smell of coffee and frying bacon was in the air. While he lay there, staring up at the ceiling and debating whether he should get out of bed, or lie there forever, Sandra came into the lean-to.

"Some men," Sandra said with pretended severity, "surely like to sleep. I'll get some snow and wash your face if you don't get up."

"O.K.," Cotton groaned. "I don't get treated with proper respect, so I might as well get up."

When he had dressed, Sandra poured his coffee, forked bacon into his plate, and put biscuits on the table before him. Cotton ate hungrily, but all the time his mind was being nudged uncomfortably by the thought that this was the time to settle something. What he wanted most of all was to rest up, eat, and have himself a time in town. Then he would ride on. Then he thought of June, he thought of Sandra, he thought of how well he liked the country, and he knew this thing of riding on was not at all what he wanted.

Sandra sat across the table from Cotton. When he had finished, she asked abruptly, "What about Ordway?"

"He won't bother you anymore," Cotton answered shortly.

"A lot of things have happened," Sandra said, "since yesterday morning. Doc got here just after you pulled out. Fred Flagg was with him, and Al Rhyman, and a couple of other men. So was the real Abernethy. Al Rhyman wanted to go after you, but Doc said it was your right to end the job. Harriman wasn't dead. He confessed that he and Donahue and Ramsay killed Luke Bray and his wife. Donahue ordered the killing because Bray had sneaked up on their campfire and heard them talking this whole scheme over. I mean about Ordway coming up, and passing himself off as Abernethy. They heard him, but he got away. They followed him to his cabin, and killed both Bray and his wife. They didn't intend to kill Mrs. Bray, but she got hit someway in the mixup. They got scared after she died, so they burned the cabin, and tried to hide the graves."

Sandra laced her slender fingers together, and placed her hands upon the table. She said, "You made a promise that you would be my foreman. I will release you from that promise. I'm going to marry J. Francis Abernethy."

Cotton rubbed a hand across his face. Then he shook his head. "I guess I'm kind o' thick-headed. What was it you said?"

"I said I'm going to marry Mr. Abernethy."

"I thought you said that." Cotton stared at her blankly. "Sandra, you haven't known the jigger long enough to know whether you want to marry him."

"Long enough. I'm making my own dicker with life, Cotton. I've been wrong about some things. The only thing I wanted was to get Malloy. That's why I made you the offer I did that first night in Antioch. From the first I knew you were the kind of fighting man I needed." She gestured wearily. "It didn't do any good. I . . . I guess I've changed. It's all in the set of values a person has. Broken Ring is mine. Mr. Abernethy likes it. He has the money to develop it. So why shouldn't I make the swap?"

"I owe you . . ." Cotton began.

"I know," Sandra said softly. "You think you owe me something. I could get you to ask me to marry you. If I said yes, and we went ahead, neither of us would be happy. That's the way the thing works, Cotton. It's no good to buck it. Life didn't deal me the cards I wanted, so I'm asking for another hand. That one I'll play. I wanted to tell you this before anyone else did. That's why I came back to the cabin. Now if I were you, I'd get on Redman, and ride to Broken Ring. That's where everybody is."

Cotton rose, and moved to the doorway. For a moment he stood there looking at Sandra, respecting her as he never had

BUCKAROO'S CODE   189

before, and feeling that he could say nothing to make her know how he felt. So, because he was a man who found it hard to put his feelings into words, he said gruffly, "Thanks for everything, Sandra. I'll be going."

She came to him, and placed a hand upon his arm. "Cotton, tell her you love her. That's the thing a woman likes to hear. I know." She hesitated. "There's one more thing. I have to confess to a lie. I did not tell June when I went to town after Doc Vance that you were asking for her."

Again Cotton felt his own inadequacy. He said, "Thanks for telling me that, Sandra," and left the cabin.

It was snowing again when Cotton reached Broken Ring. Santiam came out of the barn, looked sharply at Cotton, but did not ask about Ordway. Instead, he said, "Bill and me and Al Rhyman are working on Broken Ring. Reckon that Abernethy hombre and Sandra are getting hitched, and they sure need help on this place. What Harriman and his outfit did about keeping Broken Ring up you could stick in your eye. We've even got to start hauling hay right off, or we'll have the blasted critters starving to death if we get a big snow."

"Who's in the house?" Cotton asked.

"Abernethy, Doc, and Fred," Santiam answered. He started to build a smoke, and suddenly added as if it had completely slipped his mind, "Oh, yeah. June's in there, too."

Cotton moved toward the house, feeling his heart pounding trip-hammer blows inside his chest. When he stepped into the big living room, and stood with his back to the door, he still felt the sledgelike blows of his heart. It would be easier to mount Redman, and ride away than to tell June he loved her.

"Howdy, son," Doc called. "Kind of cold, ain't it?"

"Getting a mite chilly," Cotton admitted.

They were seated around the fireplace; Abernethy, Vance, Fred Flagg, and June. Abernethy waved toward a chair. "Sit down, Drennan. How did you make out with this man who claimed he was me?"

"He's not here," Cotton said stiffly.

Abernethy gave him a quick look, not understanding. It was Doc who said, "I don't reckon Ordway will bother you none, Abby. Fact is, I look for considerable peace now that you and Fred have got together."

Abernethy sighed. "No more fighting. No more trouble." Again he looked sharply at Cotton. "Miss Taney and I are getting married. Or perhaps you stopped at the cabin and she told you."

"Yes." Cotton nodded. "That's fine."

Abernethy looked relieved as if he had not been sure how Cotton would take it. He said, "From what I hear about you, Drennan, you're a one-man army. Now I have plans, and I'm sure they agree with what Miss Taney has in mind. I want a good cattle ranch here. I want a place where I may invite my brother Pierce and our friends, and be proud of it." He waved his hand around the room. "This is exactly what I want, but Santiam tells me the ranch has been let go back a great deal." He cleared his throat, still eying Cotton. He said bluntly, "Drennan, I'm offering you the job of being foreman here, and I assure you you'll have a free hand."

Cotton blinked. He had thought of asking for a job, but he had not expected this. He looked at June. She smiled at him, and for apparently no reason at all, rose, and walked to the other end of the big room.

"What do you say?" Abernethy asked. "I'll make this job worth your while. I know I'm getting a good man, and I'm willing to pay for him."

"I'll think it over," Cotton answered huskily. He got up, and moved to where June stood beside the window.

"It is a good job he's offering you," June said, eyes traveling the long length of him. "You can make a fine spread with his money and your savvy."

Cotton took a deep breath. "Don't make much sense to get the things a man wants unless he's got somebody to . . . to . . . well, sort of make it partners. We ain't been getting along so

BUCKAROO'S CODE   191

well lately. You thought I was doing Malloy's dirty chores, but I wasn't. You thought . . ."

June reached up and put her hand over his mouth, her dark blue eyes troubled. "Let's not go back over that," she whispered. "I know what I said. I have regretted those words every waking moment since. I know now, and I didn't know then, what a fighting man can do. The fine part of it is the fight was not entirely yours. It was ours and all of White River range. You lived by your code, Cotton, and no buckaroo ever had a finer one. That's why Abernethy is willing to trust you. I heard him talking before you came in. From what he said the ranch might as well be yours if you'll take the job."

"About what you said when we was in the cave under your cabin," Cotton went on resolutely. "And when I talked to you in the hotel . . ."

"Must we go over that again?" June asked. "I'm sorry. I can't unsay the words. When we were in the cave under the cabin I thought Dad was dying. I wasn't seeing things straight. I didn't trust Malloy, and I was afraid you were believing him. It's all over now, Cotton." She motioned outside. "It is fitting that it should snow now, Cotton. It sort of . . . well, I guess you'd say it covers up the evil that has been here for so long. Everything is changed now. Can't we forget those things I should never have said? Can't we go on from here?"

Cotton thought again of Luke Bray and his wife, and the dreams they had had. He thought of his own remark that he would like to grow up with the country, that fifty years from now he would like to attend the oldtimers' convention, and tell them how it happened. He looked down at the top of June's brown-haired head, and took another deep breath.

"I've got no right to ask this," he said, "seeing as I don't own a thing but my saddle, a roan horse, and the shirt on my back, but seems like I've got a good job. I . . . I love you. Will you marry me?"

"Oh, Cotton, I thought you were never . . ." June blushed then, and did not finish her sentence. Instead she added, "The answer is yes, and this business about you owning nothing but a roan horse, a saddle, and a shirt on your back is silly. That's all anybody needs when they start."

For a moment he stood looking at this girl he had loved for so long. Somehow it did not seem possible that it really was the way it was. Then, as he drew her to him and kissed her, he knew that this was reality, and somehow it made the things that were behind him worth some of the cost.

At the other end of the big room the rumble of talk ceased. Then Fred Flagg sighed gustily. "Watching him kiss her reminds me of when I popped the question to my missus. She was just like June, but I reckon my gal's getting a dang sight better man than my missus did."

"In a land where there are many good men," Abernethy said thoughtfully, "that man is the best."

"A good man," Doc Vance murmured, "and a good woman. What more could any country ask for?" He smiled a little then. "I reckon that's one of the things he was fighting for, and, boys, just offhand, I can't think of anything better."